"It's nice to ..."

Irritation prickled ... turned on George, not even attempting to disguise his disapproval. "You expect me to believe this *teenager* is qualified to help my son?"

A splash of rosy color bled through her cheeks. George placed a large hand on her shoulder, whether to comfort her or warn her, Nathan wasn't sure.

"Paige has almost finished her master's degree in psychology, including courses in grief counseling. I wouldn't recommend her if I wasn't confident in her abilities."

She lifted her chin and crossed her arms, as if prepared for battle. "I don't have any formal experience, but I have worked with children for years. In addition, I have an undergraduate degree in child psychology. I'm willing to meet your son and at least do an initial assessment."

Her direct gaze caused him to squirm. He wasn't usually so rude. He wasn't usually such a mess either. The nautical clock on George's desk ticked out the seconds while Nathan fought an internal debate. He looked from one to the other and finally released a long breath. "I guess we've got nothing to lose."

Susan Anne Mason lives in a suburb near Toronto, Ontario, Canada, where she works part-time as a church secretary. She is married with two amazing kids, and is a member of American Christian Fiction Writers (ACFW) and Romance Writers of America (RWA). In addition to writing, she likes to scrapbook and to research her family history online. You can connect with her on Facebook or on her website: susanannemason.com.

Books by Susan Anne Mason

Love Inspired

Healing the Widower's Heart

Healing the Widower's Heart

Susan Anne Mason

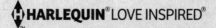
HARLEQUIN® LOVE INSPIRED®

Recycling programs
for this product may
not exist in your area.

™ LOVE INSPIRED BOOKS

ISBN-13: 978-0-373-87941-0

Healing the Widower's Heart

www.Harlequin.com

Printed in U.S.A.

If I have the gift of prophecy and can fathom all
mysteries and all knowledge, and if I have a faith
that can move mountains, but do not have love,
I am nothing.
—*1 Corinthians* 13:2

To my family,
who put up with my long hours on the laptop,
burned dinners and a mom who talks to herself!

Acknowledgments

I want to thank my wonderful critique partners, Julie, CJ and Eileen, who helped make this a better story. I also want to send a huge hug of gratitude to the awesome ladies at the Seekerville blog for sponsoring a contest that eventually led to this contract! In particular, a big thank-you to Tina Radcliffe, who gave me a cyber "kick in the pants" to enter the contest, to Ruth Logan Herne, who offered to read the whole manuscript before I submitted it, and to Julie Lessman for being my prayer warrior. Thank you all for sharing your generous hearts and your gracious spirits!

And finally, I must acknowledge my fabulous editor, Elizabeth Mazer. Thank you for loving Paige and Nathan's story! Your edits and suggestions helped make my book so much stronger. I am particularly grateful for all the compliments and happy faces you included in your edits. It did wonders for my writer's heart! :-)

Chapter One

Paige McFarlane paced the patterned carpet of the front office, her fingers clenched in the pockets of her khaki shorts. How could George put her in this position?

Seated behind his mahogany desk, the burly manager of Wyndermere House tapped a pen on his blotter. "A seven-year-old boy desperately needs your help, Paige. His father is a longtime customer, as well as a personal friend. You'd be doing us both a big favor, not to mention helping a child."

Paige stopped to face her employer and friend, trying hard not to picture a devastated little boy grieving the loss of his mother. Trying hard not to allow memories of her own horrific loss creep back into her consciousness. "My heart goes out to him, George, but I have no practical experience in grief counseling. He deserves a qualified professional."

George Reynolds's bushy eyebrows snagged in the middle of his broad forehead. "They tried that already, but it didn't work out."

Perspiration dampened Paige's palms as she fought the beginning of panic. "I'm not sure this would even be ethical since I haven't earned my certification yet." *I'm not ready for this.*

"Don't worry. I'll make it clear that you'd treat Zach more in the capacity of a camp counselor."

Paige noted the pleading gleam in her boss's brown eyes,

and felt her resolve slipping. Why was she always such a sucker for someone needing help? She really should practice saying no more often. *Psychology student, heal thyself.*

"Zach is already enrolled in your Bible camp, so you'll have lots of time together." He fixed her with a pensive stare. "You could use some extra money for school, right?"

Paige winced. Understatement of the year—not to mention a low blow. George knew she was scraping together every last penny for her final year of her master's degree.

"You know I could," she said quietly.

George swiveled in his leather chair. "Why not look at this as an opportunity to make some cash on the side then?"

"I don't know, George…" She twisted a loose strand of blond hair around her index finger, doubts wreaking havoc with her desire to help. Textbooks were all well and good, but could she honestly say she was ready to handle a troubled boy's grief? What if she made a mistake and compounded the problem?

"I wouldn't ask if I wasn't confident you could help."

Paige groaned and dropped back into the guest chair. George had been her boss since she'd started working at Wyndermere House in her teens, and he knew all too well how to use her weaknesses against her.

"Will you at least meet Nate and Zach and see how you feel? They arrive tomorrow morning, which will give you a couple of days before camp starts."

He looked so hopeful Paige didn't have the heart to say no. And the extra money wouldn't hurt.

"Fine." She threw up her hands in defeat. "I'll meet them. But I can't promise any more than that."

His smile created wrinkles around his eyes. "Thanks, kiddo. I knew I could count on you."

Good old Paige. Everyone could always count on her. She sighed a few minutes later as she pushed out the employees' entrance onto the wraparound porch. What had she gotten herself into? This could be a huge disaster in the making.

She paused to lean against the stone wall, taking in the view of the velvet lawn sloping toward the lake, and allowed the beauty of God's handiwork to steady her. The tension in her shoulder muscles eased a fraction.

Other than her hometown of Portsmouth, New Jersey, the Finger Lakes region of New York rated as close to perfection as Paige could imagine. She'd been coming here during the summer for as long as she could remember— first on vacation with her family, and later as an activity coordinator for children. She loved everything about Wyndermere House—the majesty of the sprawling stone inn, the breathtaking scenery surrounding it and most of all, the wonderful people who'd become like family.

George and Catherine Reynolds had turned this beautiful setting into a five-star resort, while using the rustic cabins farther back on the property as a summer camp for kids. Parents could leave their children under the counselors' care and partake of the resort's amenities, knowing their kids were having a blast at camp.

Paige reached into her pocket for her sunglasses, and her fingers brushed the envelope she'd hastily stuffed there before her meeting with George. Immediate tension cinched her spine as she recalled the message typed inside. *"Second installment of tuition fees due."*

Paige unclenched her fingers and released the envelope. Maybe God was giving her a gentle nudge—an opportunity to increase her finances, as well as a way to ease into the type of work she wanted to do. Still, she couldn't quite quell her anxiety. Would she be able to treat this boy without falling victim to the paralyzing emotions that had engulfed her after Colin's death?

Was she brave enough to try?

* * *

Nathan Porter scowled over the massive desk at George and bit back the words that burned on his tongue. Despite his friend's good intentions, George was meddling where he didn't belong.

"Look, Nate, you can't give up on counseling. From what you've told me, Zach's behavior is getting worse."

Nathan scrubbed a hand over his jaw. "We tried therapy and got nowhere. Zach hated every minute of it, and other than yelling obscenities at the therapist, refused to say a word. I came here for a break from all that."

"So you're going to do what? Hide from your problems all summer?"

Nathan clamped his mouth shut to rein in his anger. He wouldn't take his ill humor out on one of his best friends. "After what I've been through, I think I deserve some time off."

"That's all well and good, but what happens in September?"

Nathan stalked over to the window, where he stared out at the large expanse of water with unseeing eyes. That simple question summed up his greatest fear. Five months after his wife's sudden death, Zach was in serious emotional turmoil. Nothing Nathan did made any difference. In fact, his efforts seemed to make matters worse. He squeezed his eyes shut for a moment. If only the pain would go away—just for a little while—maybe Nathan could think clearly again.

A warm hand squeezed Nathan's shoulder. "Are your in-laws still on your back?"

"They're threatening to sue for custody if things haven't improved by September." He stuffed his hands in his pockets. "Apparently they called the school and found out Zach had been suspended for fighting. And they know I'm still not working—which gives them two good excuses to claim I'm an unfit parent."

George leaned a shoulder against the window frame. "Then why not see if Paige can get through to Zach? You'll be no worse off."

Nathan clenched his teeth, his idea for a peaceful respite slipping away as surely as his control over his life had. He closed his eyes for a moment, before turning to face his old friend. "I guess it wouldn't hurt to meet her."

"Great. I knew you'd come around to my way of thinking."

Nathan shot George a stern look. "I have one condition. I'd like to keep my profession out of this."

George frowned. "I don't see what—"

"Take it or leave it." Nathan's deep humiliation over his inability to work for the past ten months was not something he wished to discuss with anyone, especially a stranger.

George shook his head. "Fine. I'll leave that part up to you." He glanced at his watch. "Paige should be here any minute. I'm sure you'll like her as much as everyone else does."

As if on cue, a knock sounded. George strode over to swing the door open. "Come on in, kid. You're right on time."

Kid was right. Nathan frowned as a slim, blonde girl entered the room. Surely this couldn't be the grief counselor. Dressed in beige shorts and a green polo shirt containing the Wyndermere logo, her hair looped back in a ponytail, she had the fresh-faced, makeup-free complexion of a high school student.

"Paige, this is my friend Nathan Porter. Nathan, our camp director, Paige McFarlane."

The girl stepped forward, a sympathetic smile on her face, and held out her hand. "It's nice to meet you, Mr. Porter. I'm so sorry to hear about your recent loss."

He took her hand, surprised by the softness of her fingers and the almost too personal squeeze she gave. Irritation prickled the back of his neck and he quickly released her hand. He turned on George, not even attempting to disguise his disapproval. "You expect me to believe this *teenager* is qualified to help my son?"

The girl stiffened, her arms clenched tight at her sides. "I'm hardly a teenager." She glared at him with cool green eyes. Her frosty tone should have deterred him, but it didn't.

"What kind of experience could you possibly have dealing with grief-stricken children? You look like you're barely out of high school yourself."

A splash of rosy color bled through her cheeks. George placed a large hand on her shoulder, whether to comfort her or warn her, Nathan wasn't sure.

"Paige has almost finished her master's degree in psychology, including courses in grief counseling. I wouldn't recommend her if I wasn't confident in her abilities."

Master's degree? A quick calculation put her age somewhere in her midtwenties—not so very far from him after all. Why wasn't that thought more comforting?

She lifted her chin and crossed her arms, as if prepared for battle. "I don't have any formal experience, but I have worked with children for years, both here and volunteering with various programs at home. In addition, I have an undergraduate degree in child psychology. I'm willing to meet your son and at least do an initial assessment. After that you can decide what is acceptable to you."

Her direct gaze caused him to squirm in his suit jacket. He wasn't usually so rude. He wasn't usually such a mess either. The nautical clock on George's desk ticked out the seconds while Nathan fought an internal debate. He looked from one to the other and finally released a long breath. "I guess we've got nothing to lose."

"Excellent." George clapped him on the back, relief softening the strain around his mouth.

Miss McFarlane looked around the room and raised a brow. "Where *is* your son? I'd like to meet him."

"With Lou in the kitchen. I'll go get him." Nathan strode out the door at top speed. Around the first corner, he stopped and sagged against the wall, laboring for air.

This was supposed to be a relaxing retreat, a time to get his life back in order. But now—like everything else around him—the situation seemed to be spinning out of his control.

George had better know what he was doing. Zach's well-being depended on it.

The moment Mr. Porter marched out of the room, Paige thrust her shaky hands in her pockets, blinking to get the man's military-like posture and the grim set of his mouth out her mind. Far from seeming appreciative of her assistance, he had turned disapproving and cold the moment she'd entered the room.

Frowning, she trained a laser stare on George. "What's with your friend? I thought he wanted my help."

George held up his hands in mock surrender. "I know Nate's a bit gruff. This tragedy has taken a toll on him, and he's not himself right now. But Nate's a good guy, trying to do what's best for his son. Give him a chance. Please?"

Paige huffed out a sigh, remembering her own debilitating grief not that long ago. She certainly hadn't been herself then, and she supposed she could give Mr. Porter the benefit of the doubt. For his son's sake, if nothing else. "All right," she grumbled. "I'll do it—for you."

"Thank you." His smile deepened the craggy lines around his mouth and eyes.

"You're welcome." She hesitated, gathering the nerve to bring up a subject she loathed. "I hate to ask you this… but I need a favor in return."

"Name it." He picked up his coffee mug from the desk and took a quick swig.

She twisted her fingers together. "Could I get an advance on my pay? Enough to cover a partial tuition payment?"

George straightened, a frown pinching his brow. "Of course. Why didn't you ask sooner? I could have had the money to you a week ago."

She sighed. "I didn't realize the next installment was due so soon. I thought I had until August."

"I'll have a check for you tomorrow."

"Thanks, George." A huge weight lifted from her shoulders. Now she'd have some breathing room until the end of the summer to pay the remainder of her fees. If she could work things out with Mr. Porter to pay her for counseling Zach, she might be able to squeak by without having to beg the bank for more loans. Paige crossed the room to perch on the edge of his desk, her mind returning to her next challenge. "So, tell me, how did you and Nathan Porter get to be friends? He's closer to my age than yours."

"I'm actually a friend of Nate's father. Jim and Nancy used to bring him here for two weeks every summer. They became like family to me. That was before I met Catherine, and they took pity on a lonely bachelor."

Paige snorted. "Yeah, right. I'll bet you had ladies beating a path to the inn."

"Well, now that you mention it." His lips snagged up in a grin.

"So you hung out with the Porters in the summer. What else?" She sensed there was more to the story.

George shrugged. "Jim was an older father and not the outdoorsy type. So I took Nate boating and fishing and taught him to swim. We...bonded."

The conversation stopped when the door opened. Nathan reappeared, tugging a child behind him. The boy stood scowling at George and Paige, his arms crossed over his striped T-shirt. His hair, a lighter version of his father's, looked as if someone had just tousled it. Probably Lou.

The jolly cook had a soft spot for kids, especially troublesome boys.

Paige's focus shifted to Nathan Porter, this time paying more attention to his appearance. With black hair that waved over his forehead, sculpted cheekbones, a strong jaw and piercing blue eyes, Nathan Porter was one of the most handsome men Paige had ever met. A pity he wasn't more pleasant. She pulled her gaze away and focused on the guy she was *really* here to see as Nathan gave the boy a nudge forward.

"Zachary, you remember Mr. Reynolds. And this is Miss McFarlane. She's in charge of the camp you'll be attending."

Taking her cue, Paige crouched in front of the still-frowning boy and smiled. "Hi, Zach. You can call me Paige."

Zach turned angry eyes on his father. "She's a girl. How's this camp going to be any fun if she's in charge?"

Nathan's dark eyebrows slammed together. "Zachary, apologize to Miss McFarlane right this minute."

Zach planted his feet more firmly on the carpet. "I won't."

"If this is the way you're going to behave, then—"

Paige rose and quickly laid her hand on the man's arm. "Mr. Porter, could I talk to Zach alone for a moment?"

Both man and boy turned furious eyes on her, and Paige stifled a sigh. She'd have her work cut out for her, if she decided to take on this challenge. Instead of clinging to the remaining parent, as was most often the case, Zach oozed anger and defiance at his father. She had to admit the unusual dynamics of this father/son relationship piqued her professional curiosity.

"I don't want to talk to her." Zach's eyes shot daggers at her while Nathan's face turned a mottled shade of red.

Drastic action was needed to defuse the situation. "Do you like animals, Zach?"

Still frowning, he shrugged.

"I thought we could go down to the barn. We have four horses. And our cat, Misty, had kittens a few weeks ago. What do you say?"

A gleam of interest lit up his brown eyes for a moment, but the scowl returned, and he clamped his mouth shut.

Paige waited a beat, then shook her head. "That's too bad. Guess I'll just leave you here with your dad and find another camper who wants to help with the animals. It was nice to meet you, Mr. Porter." She started toward the door, ignoring the looks of disbelief on George's and Nathan Porter's faces.

"Wait." Zach's voice rang with desperation.

Hand on the doorknob, her back to the boy, Paige's lips twitched in victory. She sobered and turned to face him. "Yes, Zach?"

"I guess going to the barn is better than hanging around here."

Paige looked to Nathan for confirmation. He only nodded, his expression hovering somewhere between frustration and bewilderment.

"Good. We'll be back later then."

Before father or son could change his mind, Paige ushered Zach out the door.

On the way to the stables, she offered silent prayers Heavenward for help with this angry boy and slowed her steps to accommodate Zach, who trudged along beside her as though she were taking him to the dentist for a filling. Hopefully the horses and kittens would provide the icebreaker she needed.

"So what's your favorite animal?" she asked as they walked, dust kicking up from the dirt path.

"Dinosaurs." He glared over at her, as if daring her to contradict his choice.

"Dinosaurs are cool. I bet you like the T. rex best."

His eyes grew wide. "How did you know?"

"Most boys love them. I like the raptors."

Zach's eyes went even wider. "You know about raptors?"

"Sure. I've seen *Jurassic Park*, like, a hundred times." She gave silent thanks for her brother's obsession with dinosaurs years earlier.

"Me, too."

"So what type of pet do you like best?"

"Dogs. But cats are okay, too." He kicked at a stone on the path.

"George and Catherine have a golden retriever named Goliath. Maybe George will bring you over to see him."

When they reached the stable, Paige grabbed the heavy wooden door that squeaked as it opened, and flipped on the overhead lights. The pungent odors of manure and hay assaulted their nostrils. Zach wrinkled his nose as he stepped inside.

"I'll show you the horses first." She led the way to a stall where a large brown head peered over the door. "This is Mabel. She's our oldest mare."

Zach hung back, scuffing the toe of his sneaker on the dirt floor. Most kids who'd never been around horses were nervous the first time they encountered one. She reached out to stroke Mabel's nose, and the animal whinnied in greeting. "She's very gentle. Would you like to pat her?"

The boy hesitated, eying the horse's big head.

"I'll show you how if you want."

Zach looked up at her, brown eyes wide and uncertain. With the harshness of his scowl finally gone, Paige caught a glimpse of the vulnerable, lost child inside. Her heart squeezed with sympathy, knowing firsthand the pain and confusion that haunted him, and at that moment, she made her decision. Despite some lingering reservations, Paige resolved to do whatever she could, not only to help Zach get over the loss of his mother, but to heal his relationship with his father, as well. Zach needed to be able to depend on the only parent he had left.

Zach held out his hand. Paige took the warm fingers in hers, still sticky from Lou's cookies, and reached up to place them on the mare's nose. When he relaxed, she moved their hands up and down until he was stroking Mabel on his own.

"I think she likes you." Paige's comment earned a wavering smile from the boy. "Maybe next time we could bring her some treats. She loves apples and carrots."

They continued down the corridor, greeting the gelding, Horatio, and two more mares, Sadie and Matilda. Zach's confidence grew with each encounter.

"Will I get to ride one?"

"Probably. Jerry usually gives everyone a riding lesson." She patted Matilda one more time and moved away from the stall.

"Who's Jerry?"

"He helps me run the camp. Mainly he's in charge of the sports and the outdoor activities." Maybe if Zach knew there'd be a male involved with the camp—that it wasn't just a bunch of girls—he'd be more excited.

"What kind of sports?"

"All kinds. Canoeing, swimming, volleyball, baseball. You name it, we play it." She smiled down at him, grateful for the small spark of interest. She'd take any opening she could get. "Let's go see if we can find Misty and her babies."

Nathan tried to relax in one of the deck chairs on the big stone porch, but his mind was consumed with Zach and how he might be behaving—or misbehaving—with Paige McFarlane. Judging from his son's initial reaction, Nathan doubted it was going well.

He stood and paced the deck, hands clasped behind his

back. Never had he felt so frustrated, so helpless. Since Cynthia's tragic death, Zach's behavior had escalated in severity, and nothing Nathan said or did seemed to make a difference. It was a double blow to him since helping people was an integral part of who he was, both personally and professionally. As a pastor, he used to pride himself on his ability to shepherd his congregation through the worst times of their lives. But that all changed the moment *his* life fell apart, crumbling his faith.

Now he seemed incapable of helping anyone—least of all himself.

His thoughts turned to Paige McFarlane, and an uneasy emotion churned in his chest. He wasn't sure what he'd expected—maybe someone with bifocals and a double chin. Certainly nothing had prepared him for her.

What kind of experience could she possibly have? Was he making a huge mistake entrusting his son's emotional well-being to someone still in school?

Nathan sighed and looked at his watch. They'd been gone for almost hour. Was that a good sign or bad? He started to say a prayer for his son, but anger rose up instead, and he pushed the thoughts away.

Praying was the last thing he could depend on. His wreck of a life proved that.

Chapter Two

Paige smiled as she watched Zach cuddle the tiny ball of orange fluff close to his chest. After a few seconds, the pitiful mews stopped and the kitten curled up to sleep, soothed by Zach's steady heartbeat. Seated beside him in the straw, Paige stroked Misty's gray head, while three other wriggling bodies struggled to find a comfortable spot against their mother.

Paige glanced over at Zach, relieved to see the tense lines of his face had relaxed. "You like the orange one best?"

"Yeah. I'd name him Willy if he were mine."

"Good name." The slight upturn of his mouth in response sent a thrill of satisfaction through her. "Do you have any pets at home?"

The hard, angry look returned. "My dad won't let me."

Paige's heart clutched, remembering how her old hound dog, Chester, had absorbed buckets of her tears after Colin died. The unconditional love of a pet might be the perfect remedy to help Zach through his grief. "That's too bad. Do you or your dad have allergies?"

He shook his head. "Dad says pets are too much trouble."

Paige held back a comment, knowing she was walking on thin ice. One wrong word and the delicate trust she'd established would collapse. "Well, while you're here, Willy can be your pet. Would you like that?"

"Really?" The tentative smile reappeared.

"Sure. But he has to stay with his mother. He's too young to leave her yet."

"I'll come and visit him here then."

"Sounds like a plan." She stood and brushed the straw off her shorts and shirt. "We'd better get back to the inn before your dad gets worried."

The scowl returned. "He won't be worried. He hates me."

Paige could only stare as Zach placed the kitten down beside its siblings. "Why would you say your dad hates you?" She closed the barn door behind them and made sure the latch had caught.

Zach shrugged, his eyes trained on the ground as he walked. "He yells at me all the time. He's always mad."

Nathan Porter didn't exactly exude a sunny disposition, but what could you expect from a man who'd just lost his wife? "Your dad's not himself right now. Sometimes when adults seem angry, they're really hiding how sad they are." Her heart ached for Nathan and his son. She remembered all too well the feeling of being mired so deep in grief she thought she'd suffocate.

"My dad's not sad. He's glad my mom's dead. Except now he's stuck with me."

Paige fought to keep her jaw from dropping. For a second time, Zach had stunned her into silence. She decided against saying anything else until she'd had a chance to talk to Nathan Porter. Something a lot deeper than grief was going on between father and son.

Something she needed to figure out before she went any further.

By two o'clock, Paige had tidied her office in anticipation of her appointment with Nathan. She'd made arrangements with George's wife, Catherine, to look after Zach while they talked. After the last piece of paper had been filed, Paige stood back to survey the small room with a twinge of dismay. The surplus metal desk, file cabinet, ancient laptop and scarred wooden credenza didn't exactly portray the professional impression she'd like. But then she'd never imagined entertaining patients here.

Still she'd done her best to cheer the place up with a couple of soft lamps, a few pieces of artwork and some pictures of her favorite moments at Wyndermere.

A sharp knock brought her back to the present. She wiped her damp palms on her shorts and exhaled. "Come in."

Nathan Porter stepped inside, his larger-than-life presence making the room seem to shrink in size. He'd changed into a casual polo shirt, navy shorts and sneakers, which made him a little less intimidating than wearing a suit and tie. Still the air crackled with a subtle tension. Too bad his attitude hadn't relaxed, as well.

"Mr. Porter. Thank you for coming. Please sit down." She indicated the chair across from her desk. As he folded his tall frame onto the chair, she prayed for the right words to reach him.

"Look, Miss McFarlane," he said curtly before she could begin, "I don't want you to feel obligated to help my son. I'm sure George coerced you into doing this."

A band of heat crept up her neck, but she lifted her chin, determined to keep a professional image. "George asked me to see what I could do for Zach, and I agreed to try."

He let out a defeated breath that matched the tired lines around his eyes. "Are you aware that professional therapists have failed to get anywhere with him?"

Was that a subtle jab that she wasn't a professional yet? She pushed back the doubts creeping in and forced a calm expression. "George mentioned it. Which is why I'd like to keep this very casual. I'll incorporate Zach's sessions with the everyday activities, so it's more natural."

Nathan nodded. "That might help." He paused. "What about…compensation for your services?"

She cringed. Money was an uncomfortable topic for her. Especially when she wasn't sure if she'd be able to get through to the boy. "Why don't we leave that until I see if I can make any headway with Zach." She gripped her hands together. "Which brings me to the reason I asked to see you. In order to help your son, I need to know exactly what I'm dealing with."

She swore she could see the walls go up around Nathan, brick by brick. He shifted on the metal chair that groaned under his weight.

"Was Zach's behavior out of line?"

"No. In fact, we got along pretty well, all things considered. But something he said made me wonder if I'm missing part of the picture."

Nathan's piercing eyes narrowed. "What did he say?"

She took a deep breath before continuing, hoping to untangle the knots in her stomach. "I'm sorry if this sounds cruel, but I'm only repeating what Zach told me. He said you hate him, you're glad his mother died and you're mad because you're 'stuck' with him." She ticked the list off on her fingers.

His mouth tightened into an even grimmer line as the color drained from his face. "You must know none of that is true."

"Of course." She kept an even tone. "What I need to know is why *Zach* believes it's true."

He threw out his hands. "How should I know what goes on in the mind of a seven-year-old?"

Paige fought to keep her manner sympathetic. "Mr. Porter, I understand you're in a terrible position—trying to cope with your own loss, while helping your child deal with his overwhelming emotions."

When there was no response, she picked up her pen and

battled the urge to tap out her nerves and frustration on the legal pad. "Zach is most likely acting out quite a bit right now—creating scenes, having tantrums. Am I close?"

Nathan looked at her with unconcealed surprise. "Very."

"This type of behavior would be difficult enough to deal with in an ordinary situation. But dealing with your own issues as well must make it almost impossible."

"Yes." The relief in his voice accentuated the release of tension in his broad shoulders.

She sensed he hadn't shared this burden with anyone— that he'd been keeping his own grief bottled up. "May I ask how your wife died?" she asked gently.

He closed his eyes for a moment, and when he opened them, pain leaped from their blue depths. "A brain aneurysm—five months ago. Zach found her when he got home from school."

"Oh, no. How awful." The thought brought the sting of tears to her eyes. "No wonder he's having such a hard time. Did he call you right away?"

Nathan looked away again. "He called his grandmother and she phoned for an ambulance. But it was too late. Cynthia had been dead for hours."

"I'm so sorry. I know how hard it is to lose a loved one… unexpectedly." She struggled with a lump in her throat as painful memories surfaced. The flashing lights of the police car spearing the rain-soaked night. The wail of the siren that matched her own wail of grief. She sucked in a deep breath and pushed the images away. She couldn't afford to relive her own sorrow every time she treated a patient.

Nathan still wouldn't quite meet her eyes. Once again, Paige sensed there was far more to the situation than he was telling her. She forged ahead to cover the awkward silence. "Right now, Zach is suffering from the classic anger associated with the grieving process. He's also experiencing severe abandonment issues. Subconsciously, Zach is testing *your* limits to see if you, too, will abandon him."

Nathan's focus riveted back to her, as though she held the secrets of the universe. When she shifted under his intense stare, the wheel on her rickety chair creaked. "It's important to keep reassuring him of your unconditional love and support. Make him understand that no matter what he does, you love him and will never leave him."

A flush moved up his neck, while his gaze slid down to his clenched hands.

Suspicion flickered. "You *have* told Zach you love him, haven't you, Mr. Porter?"

"I'm his father. He knows how I feel."

She leaned forward over the desk to emphasize her point. "Everyone needs to hear the words—no matter how much you think it's understood. Especially children."

Visibly agitated, Nathan stood to pace the small enclosure. "It's not easy to profess love to a child who constantly screams 'I hate you.'"

Compassion welled within her, and inexplicably Paige found herself wanting to comfort this man, to ease his pain in some small way.

"Of course it isn't easy," she said. "But you, as the adult, have to rise above his outbursts. Sometimes a simple hug during a tantrum will defuse the situation. And right now Zach needs all the hugs he can get."

Nathan stopped pacing, his back to her. His rigid stance and lack of response told Paige there was something much deeper blocking his relationship with his son.

She jotted down a few notes on her pad of paper before posing another difficult question. "I have to ask, Mr. Porter…were there problems in your marriage?"

His back muscles visibly stiffened before he turned to pin her with an icy glare. "That is a very personal question, Miss McFarlane. And quite presumptuous, I might add."

Heat crept into her cheeks, but she didn't allow her gaze to falter. "If you want to help Zach, you need to be honest about the state of your relationship, both before and after your wife's death."

Paige could almost feel the war of emotions surging underneath the surface as Nathan contemplated her words. Finally, his shoulders slumped, and his whole body seemed to deflate. "I will do whatever it takes to help my son."

She offered him a smile of encouragement as he resumed his seat, and waited for him to speak.

He stared at the floor for several moments, then at last raised his head to look at her. "Cynthia and I separated six months before she died."

Paige's stomach dipped. Poor Zach. How much upheaval had he endured in his young life? "I see." She schooled her expression, hoping her dismay didn't show. "Was Zach living with his mother during this time?"

"Yes. She moved out and got an apartment."

Odd. Usually the mother and child stayed in the family home. "How often did you get to see Zach during the separation?"

Again Nathan's gaze slid away. "About once a month."

Paige blinked. "Why so little?"

She thought she might be the recipient of another glare, but he only sighed. "Sometimes Cynthia would cancel our weekend plans at the last minute. Sometimes an emergency would come up at work, and I'd have to cancel. It was hard to keep our schedules straight."

Paige's heart went out to the poor child caught up in that type of ping-pong match. "I imagine Zach's behavior was less than ideal during your allotted visits."

One dark eyebrow rose. "That's an understatement."

"Which made you dread the time you spent with him instead of looking forward to it."

"Pretty much."

Now they were getting somewhere. "I'd like you to look at your separation from Zach's point of view for a minute. His mother takes him away from his home, from everything familiar. Then every time his dad is supposed to come and see him, the plans fall apart. And when they do spend time together, his father seems like he can't wait to leave. Zach comes to the conclusion that his father doesn't want to see him and doesn't care about him. A lot of anger and resentment builds up. Compound that with his mother's sudden death, and quite frankly I'm surprised Zach's not a lot worse off than he is."

Nathan's silence spoke volumes. She decided not to push for anything further at this point. "Thank you, Mr. Porter. I have a much better understanding of Zach's emotional state now. I should be able to help him work through some issues. May I ask how long you're planning to stay at Wyndermere?"

"I haven't decided. A month—maybe more. But Zach will attend camp the whole summer."

He pinched the bridge of his nose as if trying to ease a headache. "There's something else you should probably know. Zach's behavior at school got him suspended twice. And Zach's maternal grandparents have threatened to sue for custody if his behavior hasn't improved by September. I don't think they'll do anything over the summer, but just in case, I wanted you to be aware."

Paige paused to digest this information. "Good to know. I'll do my best to help Zach and will keep you informed on his progress." She rose and offered her hand, praying he couldn't tell that she felt as off-kilter as a new colt.

In one fluid motion, he stood and engulfed her palm in his. A tremor raced up her arm as his intense gaze held hers. The stark sorrow in their depths stalled the air in her lungs.

"I'll be grateful for any improvement you can bring about, Miss McFarlane."

With a slight nod, he released her hand and quietly left the room.

Paige slumped into her chair and let the air whoosh out of her lungs as she lifted a silent plea Heavenward. Without divine assistance, she feared she would never be able to heal the broken spirits of either Zach or his father.

The fresh air came as a relief after the confinement of Paige McFarlane's office. Nathan's long strides ate up the path as he headed toward the lake, consumed with the need for physical activity to release his pent-up emotions.

As he followed the lakeside, his brisk walk changed to a jog. He focused on the air rushing in and out of his lungs, and the sting of his leg muscles, allowing the sensations to block out all the negative emotions that had started to surface during his talk with that woman. He needed the exertion to push them firmly back where they belonged.

Winded, he stopped to lean against a tree and stared out over the water. The serenity of the scene did nothing to ease his anxiety. His mind was in chaos, his emotions churning. Talking about his marital difficulties had brought all the guilt and anger rushing back to the surface—a toxic mixture that had all but crippled his life in New York and rendered him incapable of continuing his ministry. His parishioners deserved someone who demonstrated a shining example of faith and courage, not a man paralyzed with hatred and bitterness.

Nathan continued on the path by the water, this time walking. Deep-breathing exercises allowed him to corral his unwanted feelings back into the appropriate compartment. It was ironic, really. His friends and family had all tried to get him to see a counselor, but he'd refused. The thought of baring his soul to a stranger, even another clergy member, made him physically ill.

Now, while trying to help his son, Paige McFarlane had

started poking into the most private areas of his life. Areas he wanted to keep buried. Somehow he had a feeling she would not allow that to happen.

He sighed, and reluctantly headed down the beach in the direction of George and Catherine's house to pick up his son, his mind still consumed by one unavoidable question.

How was he ever going to help Zach when he was powerless to help himself?

Paige entered the employee cafeteria on the lower level of the inn, grateful for a distraction from her thoughts of Nathan and Zach's problems. She found Jerry already seated at their usual table, two trays in front of him. With his sandy brown hair and freckles, Jerry Walton appeared a lot younger than his twenty-five years. He hadn't changed a bit since they'd started running the children's camp at Wyndermere four years earlier.

"You're late. I got you a burger. Hope that's okay."

"Perfect. I'm starving." She threw her files on the table and plopped onto a chair.

Jerry wiped a drip of mustard from his mouth. "Any word from Sandy? I thought she'd be here by now."

Paige scanned the bustling room as if Sandy Bennett, the third member of their team, would materialize. "Not yet. I know she expected to arrive late, but I thought she'd be here by now."

Jerry shrugged. "No use wasting time. Let's go over the schedule again."

Paige chewed a large bite of her burger and opened her folder. Everything was falling into place for the camp, at least on paper. Dealing with the reality of the children would be a whole different dynamic.

"How'd your meeting go with Zach's father?"

Paige shrugged. "Not bad. I learned some background information that will be helpful." She set her burger down with a sigh. "I'm still not sure I'm doing the right thing, Jer. I might be in way over my head."

He raised a brow. "What's the worst that could happen? If you get nowhere with the kid, his father will have to take him somewhere else. In the meantime, he's going to have a great time here."

Despite her uneasiness, Paige couldn't help but smile. "I guess you're right. Being at Wyndermere always made me feel better, no matter what was going on in my life." Even when her own grief had weighed her down.

"Okay, it's settled. Now, can we get to work here? We've got a ton to do before the kids arrive tomorrow."

"Got the plan of attack all worked out?"

Paige looked up at the familiar voice and broke into a wide smile. "Sandy. You made it." She jumped up to embrace the petite brunette. "When did you get in?"

"About an hour ago." Sandy gave Jerry a quick hug and dropped into a chair at their table. "Sorry it's so last-minute. Being maid of honor for my sister was exhausting." Her easy grin and cheerful demeanor brightened the room. "It's good to see you guys."

"Same here." Paige resumed her seat, already feeling steadier now that her friend had arrived. "You look great. I like the new do."

Sandy swung her head so that her layered brown hair moved with the breeze. The shorter feathered cut suited her big blue eyes and pixie face.

"A makeover for the wedding."

"If you guys are going to trade beauty secrets, I'm out of here," Jerry grumbled.

"Relax." Sandy patted his cheek. "We'll catch up on the girl talk later. Right now I need a crash course on tomorrow's schedule."

While Jerry filled Sandy in on the details, Paige went to get another round of iced tea. Thankfully, the cafeteria crowd had thinned out, which meant a quieter noise level for their meeting. She was on her way back with a tray of drinks when a tall figure blocked her path.

"Hey, gorgeous. Let me get that for you."

Brandon Marshall, one of the students from last summer who did maintenance around the grounds, took the tray out of her hands and grinned down at her. His longish brown hair skimmed bold eyes that raked over her.

Paige swallowed her dismay. She'd hoped Brandon wouldn't be back this year. His arrogance had always rubbed her the wrong way. "Hello, Brandon. How are you?"

If he noticed her less than enthusiastic greeting, he ignored it. "Fantastic, now that I've seen you."

He flashed a rakish smile, which only annoyed her further. She'd spent most of last summer fending off his attention, and it looked as if things would be no different this year. Reluctantly, she led him to her table, where he set the drinks down with a flourish.

She nodded at her friends. "You remember Jerry and Sandy?"

"Yeah, sure." He barely glanced in their direction.

Not wanting to appear rude, she asked if Brandon would like to join them.

"No, thanks. I've got somewhere to be. But I'll be seeing *you* around." He winked at her as he backed out of the room.

Paige dropped into her chair with a grimace.

Sandy crossed her arms. "Looks like Romeo's on the prowl again. You're going to have to say something if you don't want a repeat of last summer."

Paige groaned. "I tried to get rid of him last year, but he wouldn't take the hint."

"Then you'll have to be more forceful, so he gets the message loud and clear."

Jerry reached for his glass. "Aw, Brandon's harmless."

Sandy shot him a disgusted look. "You men always stick

together, don't you?" She stabbed her pen in the air. "Seriously, Paige, be careful. Something about Brandon gives me bad vibes."

As they settled back to work, Paige hoped Sandy's instincts were wrong. With everything else on her plate—initiating the new camp program, helping Zach Porter, struggling to figure out how she'd make ends meet for her last year of grad school—she didn't need the added aggravation of fending off unwanted male attention.

Especially since her plans for the future did not include romance. She'd learned the hard way what loving someone—and losing them—could cost, and she'd vowed to never let that happen again.

Chapter Three

"Have you ever been in a canoe before, Zach?"

Kneeling on the dock, Paige adjusted the belt on the boy's life jacket. With a few hours left of daylight, Paige had opted to have a little one-on-one time with Zach before the hectic first day of camp the next morning. Nathan had seemed relieved at her offer to spend time with Zach and had politely declined her invitation to join them.

The fact that Zach had agreed to come with her only after she'd bribed him with ice cream did not bode well for their talk. Paige hoped that being out on the water for an impromptu canoe lesson would work in her favor, as opposed to keeping Zach cooped up in her dungeon of an office. Paige sighed, wondering again how she'd gotten roped into this crazy situation.

"I went canoeing once with my cousins on a camping trip." Zach kicked at a stone on the dock.

Paige rose and offered a smile of encouragement. "Good. Then you know how easy it is to tip a canoe and how careful you have to be to balance the boat."

"I guess." Zach tugged on the zipper of his jacket. "Do I have to wear this thing? I can swim, you know."

"Everyone has to wear a life jacket no matter how well they can swim. It's a Wyndermere rule." Paige held the side of the canoe and motioned for Zach to board. "Nice and slow and stay low toward the bottom of the boat."

Zach stepped inside, wobbled for a second before re-gaining his balance and then scrambled to one of the seats.

Paige steadied the craft and got in herself, opting to kneel on one of the floatation cushions. Using one of the paddles, she pushed away from the dock. The boat glided out into the lake. "I'll get us out a bit farther before I show you how to row."

Zach nodded. He peered out over the smooth water and pointed. "Can we go all the way to that island?"

"Not tonight. That's pretty far out."

Zach scowled at her. "It doesn't look that far."

Paige mentally counted to ten. Zach seemed prepared to challenge her every statement. "Let's take it one step at a time." She began paddling in a rhythmic pattern and headed toward the open water. A light breeze teased the ends of her hair, cool enough to make her glad she'd worn a sweatshirt.

"When are the other camp kids getting here?" The brim of Zach's cap almost hid his eyes, but Paige had no trou-ble telling that they were hard and closed-off. She had a feeling he was less interested in meeting new people and more interested in her being too distracted by the others to bother him.

"Some arrived today. A few will come tomorrow morn-ing in time to register." She paused for a moment to adjust the brim of her Wyndermere cap to block the sun. Even her sunglasses couldn't reflect the glare off the water. "Are you looking forward to moving into the cabins?" Zach had been staying in Nathan's suite at the inn, but would be joining the rest of the campers tomorrow at the two cab-ins near the woods.

"Yeah. As long as the kids aren't lame."

Paige hoped the scowl lines weren't permanently grooved into the boy's face. "No one is lame, Zach. And I'll tell you right now that everyone is expected to get along.

You may not like every boy or girl you meet, but you will treat them with politeness and respect. And they will treat you the same way."

Zach pressed his mouth into a thin line and shrugged. "Whatever."

Paige bit back a rebuke and decided to change focus. "You ready to try paddling?"

He nodded and she handed him a paddle. She positioned his hands on the tool and gave him some basic pointers on how to use the blade. Soon he had mastered the technique and was moving the canoe forward.

"You're doing great," she told him. "Next time I'll teach you how to steer."

They floated along in silence for several minutes until Paige figured they'd better start heading back. "I'll turn us around. The sun will almost be down by the time we get back."

"All right. I guess it *is* too far to get to the island."

She smiled. "It's a lot farther than it looks." Expertly she guided the canoe around. "So where do you live, Zach?" Paige opted to begin the counseling by asking a few harmless questions to get Zach used to talking with her.

"In New York."

"Do you like your school?"

"It's okay." He turned his face slightly and stared over her shoulder.

"What do you do for fun? Play any sports?"

His shoulders relaxed a fraction. "In the summer, I play baseball and soccer. Except this year I won't because I'm here."

Sheesh. Every question was like entering a minefield. "Don't worry. We'll be playing a lot of sports, too."

He shrugged and kept staring at the horizon. Farther out, a speedboat flew by, creating a ripple of waves.

"While you're here, you and I are going to spend some

time talking." If she were lucky, Zach wouldn't dive over-
board.

The paddle splashed the surface of the water, sending a
spray of moisture over them. "Talking about what?"

She exhaled slowly. "About your mom and your relationship with your dad. I noticed you don't seem to be getting along too well."

Zach fumbled and nearly dropped the paddle over the
side. Paige reached out to steady it.

The boy's eyes glinted with anger. "I don't want to talk
about that stuff."

Paige dipped her paddle into the water, grateful the
Wyndermere dock was now in sight. "I understand it's difficult. We'll take it really slow, a little at a time, until you
feel more comfortable."

With a grunt, Zach lurched to his feet and heaved his
paddle out into the lake. The canoe shuddered with the sudden movement, and before Paige could counter the momentum, the boat flipped, sending her tumbling into the water.

What was Zach doing standing in the canoe? From his
position at the end of the dock, Nathan watched in horror
as Zach teetered, waving his arms in a futile attempt to
regain his balance, and then plunged into the water with
a large splash. The boat quickly followed suit, upending
Paige and the equipment into the lake.

Nathan checked the strong urge to dive into the water
and rescue them, realizing that this was part of the woman's job. Surely it wasn't the first time a camper had cap-
sized a canoe.

In seconds, her dripping head broke the surface. Nathan
was gratified to see that she swam directly to Zach and
made sure he was all right, before righting the canoe and
salvaging the paddles and a flotation device. She helped
Zach back into the craft and then swam beside it, effec-

tively towing them until her feet reached the bottom and she could stand.

From the angry scowl on Zach's face, Nathan surmised the outing had not gone well. Paige headed to the beach. Nathan made his way down from the dock to help her drag the canoe onto the sand. She pushed wet strands of hair off her forehead, avoiding his eyes.

"What happened out there?" Nathan asked, lending Zach a hand to climb out. His son's clothes were drenched and his cap was missing.

"Nothing." Zach pushed away from him as soon as his feet hit the sand, and he trudged up the beach, leaving wet footprints in his wake.

"Not nothing." Paige's head snapped up and she took off after Zach. "Wait a minute, Zach."

He kept going. Nathan followed, a feeling of dread dogging his footsteps.

Paige ran in front of Zach and put a hand on his shoulder, her mouth turned down. "That was a very foolish thing to do. You could have been badly hurt if that canoe had landed on you."

Zach wrenched his arm away, glaring.

Nathan held back a groan of frustration. Camp hadn't even begun and already Zach had alienated the director. "What did Zach do?"

Paige straightened and looked at Nathan. "He stood up and caused the boat to tip. A common mistake made by first-time canoers." She turned her gaze back to Zach, who shivered in the cool evening breeze. "I just want to make sure he understands the dangers involved, so he won't do it again."

Zach lowered his head. "Sorry," he mumbled.

Paige's posture relaxed. "That's okay. You'd better go get changed. I'll see you bright and early tomorrow for the start of camp."

Zach nodded, and for the first time looked at his father. Nathan held back the reprimand on his tongue. He'd save that for later. "Go on up to the room and start the shower. I'll be right there."

Without another word, Zach turned and headed toward the inn.

Nathan followed Paige back to the canoe and helped her dump out the water. They left it upside down on the beach to dry.

She folded her arms across her chest, a worried expression darkening her eyes. "I'm afraid we didn't get off to a great start."

His instincts had been right then. "What really happened?"

She bit her bottom lip. "When I told Zach that I would be talking to him about his mother, he got upset."

"And?"

"He jumped up and threw one of the paddles out into the lake." She sounded apologetic as if she was the one who had done something wrong. "Maybe I brought it up too abruptly."

She shivered, and he realized she must be freezing. The sun had dipped below the horizon of the lake and even in dry clothes, he was aware of a cool breeze off the water. "You should go get changed yourself."

She nodded. "Hopefully things will go better tomorrow."

He gave her one last look and shook his head. "From past experience, I wouldn't count on it. Good night, Miss McFarlane."

She let out a soft sigh. "Good night, Mr. Porter."

Monday morning, Paige bit down on her pen as she double-checked the list of names on her clipboard. All the campers except one had arrived. She glanced at her watch.

Nine fifteen. She'd waited long enough. Time to start the orientation.

As was the tradition every first morning of camp, Paige put on a little welcome for the children and their families. It was a good way to help everyone feel more comfortable. Once the kids got to meet each other, the parents could say their goodbyes and discreetly leave.

Paige raised her head to scan the group of people socializing on the stone patio. It was the perfect weather to hold the event outdoors today. Lou had provided a light buffet-style breakfast with fresh orange juice, fruit and an assortment of pastries. Some of the kids had already paired up. The girls especially stood grouped together, comparing backpacks. Jerry demonstrated some volleyball moves to the boys, while the parents mingled by the coffee bar.

All except Nathan Porter, who stood alone by the far wall, sunglasses hiding his eyes. From the grim set of his mouth, he didn't seem at all happy to be here. If Paige hadn't emphasized the necessity for all parents to participate, she had little doubt he would have remained in his room—alone. At least Zach was mixing with the other boys. Paige prayed he'd make friends easily. That would play a huge role in whether or not he would enjoy the camp experience.

A boy and a woman came into sight, walking hesitantly across the patio toward the crowd.

Ah, the missing camper. Paige strode toward them. The dark-haired woman placed a hand on the boy's shoulder as Paige approached.

"Hello. This must be Peter." Paige smiled at the boy.

His blue eyes, framed by black-rimmed glasses, regarded her with a serious gaze.

"Yes," the woman answered. "I'm Anna O'Brien, Peter's mom. Sorry we're late. I got lost on those side roads." An air of sadness hugged the woman's features.

"I'm Paige McFarlane, the camp director. Please come and join the rest of us. We have refreshments and coffee on the far table, and we'll begin the orientation tour in about ten minutes." Paige wanted to give the newcomers time to meet the others before they started. She ushered the pair over to the group, guiding Peter toward the other boys.

"Hey, guys. This is Peter. Peter, these are some of the other campers. There's Justin, Bobby, Steven, Kyle and Zach."

"Hi." Kyle came forward to greet Peter. He glanced at Peter's mom hovering behind Paige.

Definitely one of the overprotective types, Paige decided.

"How come your dad didn't come?" Kyle asked. "Both my parents are here."

Peter shifted from one sneaker to the other. From the corner of her eye, Paige saw Anna stiffen.

"My dad's dead." Peter shrugged. "He died in Iraq."

Paige gripped her clipboard tighter. Another child who'd lost a parent. Was she destined to open Wyndermere's Center for Grieving Children?

Kyle scratched his elbow. "Oh, sorry. I thought maybe your parents were divorced like Bobby's."

Anna stepped up beside Paige. "I was going to tell you privately," she said in a quiet voice. "It happened almost a year ago, but Peter can still be withdrawn sometimes."

Paige gave her arm a sympathetic squeeze. "Thank you for letting me know. I'll take extra care with him."

The woman's eyes moistened. "Thank you."

At the same time, Paige noticed Zach moving closer, his hands stuffed in the pockets of his shorts.

"My mom's dead, too."

Paige held her breath as Zach looked right at Peter. The whole group seemed to stop talking as if awaiting the boy's reaction.

Peter pushed his glasses up higher on his nose. "Guess we're both half orphans."

"Guess so." Zach pointed to the table of food. "Wanna go get something to eat? The muffins are awesome."

"Sure."

As the boys moved off, Paige let out the breath she'd been holding. *Lord, You sure answer prayers in unique ways sometimes. Thank You for bringing Peter here for Zach. I think he's just the friend Zach needs.*

Chapter Four

"Who can tell me the main point in the story of the prodigal son?" Paige smiled at the twelve eager faces in the meeting room they used as a classroom during camp every summer.

Three days in, and apart from a few minor glitches, the program had been running smoothly. The kids were bright, eager and, for the most part, well behaved. Even Zach had settled in to camp life without incident, due in large part, Page felt, to his budding friendship with Peter. The two had been inseparable since the first morning.

Her gaze settled on Zach and her stomach nose-dived. Make that eleven eager faces and one scowling one. She turned her attention to the four hands waving wildly in the air. "Yes, Felicia?"

The girl's beaming smile revealed several missing teeth. "If you do bad things but you're sorry, your parents will forgive you."

"Very good. Forgiveness is the moral of our story. Like the father in the parable, our Heavenly Father forgives all our sins if we are truly sorry. He'll always be waiting for us if we decide to come back to Him." She looked at the clock. "That's all the time we have for now. I want you all to think about which Bible story you'd like to study on Friday, and we'll vote on it tomorrow. Now everyone down to the lake."

A flurry of activity ensued as the group rushed to follow Sandy, eager for their canoe lesson with Jerry. Zach, however, remained in his seat, glaring at the tabletop. Peter hovered in the doorway as though unsure what to do.

"You go on with the others, Peter. Zach will be out in a minute."

Peter nodded and dashed off to catch up with the campers, his footsteps echoing down the corridor.

Paige turned to study Zach's profile, and huffed out a small sigh. She hadn't made any progress with him over the past few days. Other than those few words he'd said to Peter, Zach remained closemouthed about anything to do with his mother. Maybe if Paige pried into whatever had caused his present bad mood, she'd get him to open up.

With casual strokes, she erased the whiteboard. "Didn't you like today's story, Zach?" She darted a glance over her shoulder.

"No." He shredded a strip off the handout she'd given everyone.

She set the eraser down. "May I ask why?"

"Because it's all a big, fat lie."

Paige allowed herself no reaction to Zach's outburst. "Which part exactly is a lie?"

Deep ridges formed between his brows. "The part about fathers always forgiving stuff. You shouldn't tell everyone they do."

He turned furious eyes on her, glittering with unshed tears. Sympathy welled in her chest, and the frustration from the past few days melted away. She longed to take him in her arms and promise him everything would be all right. But that would be totally unprofessional and totally unacceptable.

First rule of therapy—no touching the patient.

She took a few steps closer and crouched beside his chair. "What won't your father forgive?" she asked softly.

Zach shrugged and rubbed a hand across his face. "Not

what—who. He wouldn't forgive my mom." He waited a minute before continuing. "She took me away, and my dad was real mad about that. But later Mom wanted us to go home again." His face crumpled, like the paper under his fingers. "She cried and said she was sorry, just like the prodigal son. But Dad didn't care. He said we couldn't come home. He hates us." His voice broke on a stifled sob.

His tears overflowed and dripped down his cheeks. Zach looked away in obvious distress, and Paige just couldn't ignore his suffering. Throwing the rules out the window, she pulled him to her and pressed his head to her shoulder. "It's okay to cry, Zach," she whispered.

She expected him to argue, even pull away. Instead he clutched at her, sobs racking his slim body while hot tears drenched her shirt. Her heart broke for this child and the soul-wrenching grief that consumed him. She stroked his tousled hair until he finally quieted. Paige found her own eyes moist when he drew away from her and wiped his face on his sleeve.

"You won't tell my dad about this, will you?"

"About what?" She frowned, then recognized the embarrassment on his face. "You mean, that you were crying?"

He nodded, not looking at her. "My dad never cries."

"I'm sure he does in private. Most dads don't like to cry in front of anyone."

Zach shook his head. "He says men don't cry."

Annoyance prickled at that kind of archaic, macho belief. "Crying is nothing to be ashamed of, honey. It helps your heart heal."

"I guess." But he didn't sound convinced.

With gentle fingers, she pushed an unruly curl off his forehead. "Anytime you feel sad or like crying, you can come to me. I'll be your safe place where you can say or do whatever you want. Okay?"

"Okay."

Her heart tumbled when he raised vulnerable eyes to hers and swiped a hand across his nose. She pulled a tissue from her pocket and handed it to him. "You ready to join the others for another canoe lesson?"

When he nodded, she held out her hand. "Come on, I'll walk you down."

With his trusting hand in hers, they made their way to the lake. Paige lifted a prayer as she walked.

Lord, please use me to be Zach's place of refuge. Let him feel safe with me and allow me to ease his pain. And while You're at it, I could use some help getting through to his father.

Secretly, Paige thought that breaking down Nathan's walls might prove to be the tougher job all around.

Nathan's footsteps echoed down the hallway outside the auditorium, where, according to the posted schedule, the children should be practicing songs for a play. He'd slip in and watch the end of the rehearsal until he could speak with Miss McFarlane.

With some effort, Nathan pushed back his resentment at another summons from the persistent woman. He hadn't really spoken to her—other than a brief hello at the opening of camp—since the canoe-tipping incident, and he suspected Zach had done something else to incur her discipline. He only hoped it wasn't serious enough for Miss McFarlane to banish Zach from the camp altogether. Though he had to admit, despite the tension between them, he missed Zach's presence in the suite they'd shared for a few days before camp started. Nathan sighed. At least, from what Nathan was able to observe, Zach seemed to be enjoying the camaraderie with other boys his age.

Nathan paused at the door to the auditorium and tugged at the collar of his polo shirt. For reasons he couldn't name, Paige McFarlane unsettled him, challenged him, made him feel like an incompetent parent. Then again, maybe it was his own insecurity talking.

In any case, he needed to put his personal feelings aside and allow her to do her job—because he couldn't deny that whether or not she'd gotten Zach to open up about his mother's death, she'd already brought about changes in his son that Nathan could not. He'd witnessed Zach interacting with the other kids, watched him laughing and playing like a normal seven-year-old. That alone was worth putting up with Miss McFarlane's superior attitude.

He placed a hand on the door handle, cracked it open an inch, then stopped to listen. A voice as pure and sweet as liquid honey floated on the air toward him. Who was that singing? Surely not one of the children. Nathan nudged the door open and slid inside. His insides quivered, resonating with the deep tone of the piano. He hadn't listened to any music since Cynthia's funeral. Music evoked too many powerful emotions—emotions he'd fought long and hard to repress.

He paused now, however, to let the beauty of the song roll over him, squinting to see whom the exquisite voice belonged to. Rendered immobile, he could only stare.

The person singing was none other than Paige McFarlane.

He stood riveted in place while her voice, as soothing as a balm, reached some secret place inside him and touched his very soul. The song ended on a poignant note, at which time the children burst into loud applause.

Nathan blinked in an effort to break the spell that had befallen him. The soft stage lights danced over Paige's pale hair, creating a quivering aura around her. Her green eyes glowed with emotion, giving her smile a euphoric quality, and for a moment, he wondered if she were real or an illusion.

A petite brunette rounded up the kids and herded them

through the door. Paige hopped down from the stage and stopped to speak to the other camp counselor—Jerry, he thought his name was—at the piano. She glanced up, and did a double take when she saw Nathan. She said something to Jerry, then started across the auditorium toward him.

Shaking his head to clear his thoughts, Nathan moved to meet her halfway. "I got your message. You wanted to see me?"

She clutched a book of music in front of her. "Thanks for coming. I didn't expect you so soon." She glanced back at Jerry, who waved on his way out. "I need to speak to you again about Zach."

Tension banded across his shoulders as memories of being summoned to the principal's office of Zach's school flew to mind. He took a deep breath. "Could we maybe talk over a cup of coffee?"

Her mouth opened and shut. She looked down at her watch. "I guess I could spare a few minutes. How about the café upstairs?"

He nodded and followed her into the corridor. An awkward silence descended as they made their way to the outdoor terrace, one of Nathan's favorite spots. Small iron tables canopied by striped umbrellas overlooked the water below, scented by baskets of hanging geraniums. Other than one other couple, the area was empty at this time of day.

Nathan pulled out a seat for Paige at a table by the low stone wall. Her long hair was loose today and flowed over her shoulders.

After they'd ordered two coffees, he leaned back against the metal chair. "That song you were singing, is it from *The Sound of Music*?"

She looked up, surprise registering in her clear eyes. "Yes, it is. We're practicing a shortened version of the play to put on for the parents."

"You have a beautiful voice."

Paige looked down and moved her book to one side, a blush staining her cheeks. "Thank you."

Maybe he was stalling, to keep her from telling him something unpleasant about Zach. Or maybe he wanted to relate to her on a more personal level, instead of as a therapist. Whatever the reason, he wanted to know more about this woman. "Where did you learn to sing like that?"

The waiter arrived and set down their cups with a brief nod to Paige. She picked up a packet of sugar. "Both my parents have musical backgrounds. My father teaches music at the high school in my hometown, and we were all involved in the church choir." She stirred her coffee, the spoon clinking against the ceramic mug. "Speaking of voices, Zach sings well for his age. Does musical talent run in your family, too?"

Nathan paused to consider her unexpected question. Other than hymns, he hadn't thought about singing in years. "I used to sing in high school and did a little college theater. In fact, I played the captain in *The Sound of Music* my senior year."

"How ironic we picked that particular piece." Her lips quirked as if she was trying not to laugh.

He had to stop looking at her mouth. He took a long sip of his coffee, enjoying the strong burst of flavor, then set down his cup. "Miss McFarlane—"

"Please, call me Paige."

"Paige then. What did you want to see me about?"

The amusement left her eyes, replaced with regret. "We had another…incident earlier. Zach got upset over a Bible lesson on forgiveness."

Nathan frowned. "Why would that upset him?"

A trace of a sigh escaped her lips. "He said you wouldn't forgive his mother and let her come home."

The coffee soured in his stomach. He hadn't realized Zach knew anything about Cynthia's request to move back home. Or that he'd refused her. That might explain some of Zach's anger toward him.

He met her curious gaze. "He's right. Cynthia did want to come back…but I couldn't let her. I couldn't take her back on a whim."

Paige bit her bottom lip, questions brimming in her eyes. "You're wondering why she left me."

She shrugged. "You don't have to tell me. I'm sure it's very personal."

"It is. But it may help with Zach." He swirled the brown liquid in his mug, choosing his next words with care. "Cynthia got tired of coming second to my career. She couldn't take my long hours and the constant demands on my time."

"Sounds like a stressful job. What do you do?"

A nerve twitched in his jaw as a vision of Saint Stephen's church rushed to mind. He was nowhere near ready to talk about his professional failure. Much too personal, much too painful. "That's not important. Suffice it to say that Cynthia grew less and less supportive. I knew she was unhappy, but I never thought she'd leave." His fingers tightened around the mug. *Might as well tell her the rest. She'll find out sooner or later.* "The ugly truth is…my wife left me for another man." The familiar surge of humiliation rose up to swamp him.

A mixture of disbelief and pity flitted across Paige's face. "I'm so sorry." She reached out a hand, but pulled it back before she made contact with his arm. "That must have been terrible for you."

"You have no idea." He gave a harsh laugh. "Then, after six months of misery, she told me she'd made a mistake and wanted to come home. Apparently her new boyfriend didn't like being tied down with a child." He shook his head. "As much as I missed Zach, I couldn't take the risk of letting her back into my home or my life. I didn't trust her anymore." He glanced over to gauge Paige's reaction. For some reason, it mattered that she understand his point of view.

A small frown creased her forehead. "Of course not. Not after what she put you through. She needed to earn your trust back again."

His shoulders sagged at the lack of censure in her voice. "Thank you for saying that." He closed his eyes against the wave of pain. "I only wish I could make myself believe that I did the right thing."

His lids flew open at the feel of her warm hand on his arm. Compassion shone in her eyes.

"You feel guilty because she died before you could resolve things between you," she said softly.

The unbearable weight of it crushed his shoulders. *If only it were that simple.* He swallowed what felt like shards of glass. "I feel guilty," he said, "because I'm responsible for her death."

Paige reeled from the shock of Nathan's words. How could that be? "I thought your wife died from a brain aneurysm."

He scrubbed a hand over his jaw. "The aneurysm happened after I refused Cynthia's request to reconcile. The doctor said stress was a significant factor in causing the rupture. I might as well have put a gun to her head." The bitterness in his voice tore at her heart.

She shifted in her chair, leaned in and squeezed his arm. "You're wrong, Nathan. You can't take the blame for Cynthia's bad choices. That type of guilt will eat you alive." Long-dormant emotions bubbled up like a geyser to flood her senses. She knew all about dealing with guilt. Guilt that ate at your soul and prevented healing.

Nathan barked out a harsh laugh. "Tell me about it."

For the first time, Paige understood the pain behind his

coldness and anger. And the reason he hadn't been able to be there for his son.

Nathan was emotionally paralyzed.

She knew this, not only from the textbooks she'd studied, but from painful, personal experience. "I understand exactly what you're going through," she said softly.

Paige had never told a stranger her story. As painful as it would be to reopen the wound, if it could benefit Nathan and Zach, how could she hold back?

She bit her lip, trying to decide if she had the courage to go through with it. Before she could make up her mind, her cell phone went off. She glanced down at the display from Jerry. "I'm sorry," she said to Nathan. "They need me down at the water."

"Of course." The shuttered look had returned.

Paige rose and gathered her music book. "Thank you for the coffee. Maybe we can continue this conversation another time." Perhaps then she'd be better prepared to share her story.

Nathan rose, as well. "I'd like that." Despite his gruffness, he seemed sincere.

She nodded and turned to descend the stone steps. It might have been her imagination, but as she made her way down to the beach, Paige could almost feel him watching her.

Chapter Five

Nathan threw the book of sudoku puzzles onto the coffee table, leaned his head back against the sofa cushions and closed his eyes, wondering exactly when he'd become a hermit. Holed up in his hotel room with an odd assortment of puzzles for company.

Nathan sighed, trying hard not to think about everyone outside celebrating the Fourth of July with a barbecue, while he ate a cold sandwich on the couch. Alone.

Part of him yearned to join in with the festivities, to forget his anguish for one night, and pretend to be someone other than a washed-up minister with a son who hated him. But no matter where Nathan went, he couldn't escape his past. Inevitably someone would ask him about his family, or his job. If only he were good at inventing vague answers. Unfortunately, the talent to fabricate stories seemed beyond his skill set.

Memories of past holidays stormed through his mind with the relentless fury of a freight train. Memories of the church picnics in the park, of families playing Frisbee, tag and hide-and-seek, waiting for the annual fireworks display to begin. Memories of happier times with Cynthia when they'd carry a sleeping Zach home to bed and tuck him in together.

Desperate for a distraction, Nathan grabbed the remote and clicked on the TV. If he were lucky, some mindless criminal show would capture his interest until it was late enough to go to bed.

He'd flicked through all the channels when a loud rap at his door startled him. He pressed the mute button and got slowly to his feet, annoyance climbing through him. Probably either George or Catherine, trying to coerce him to come out. His friends meant well, but couldn't they understand he'd come up here for solitude and quiet?

A second knock, louder this time, echoed in the room.

"Who is it?"

"Paige McFarlane."

Nathan jolted to his full height. What was she doing here? He flung open the door.

Dressed in her usual Wyndermere polo shirt and jeans, her hair loose around her shoulders, Paige stood poised ready to knock again.

"Is Zach okay?" he practically barked at her.

"He's fine." Her citrus scent swirled around him, irritating his already foul mood even further.

"Then why are you here?" Maybe if he was rude enough, she'd leave him be.

Instead, she hiked her chin, green eyes flashing. "I wondered why you weren't attending the celebration with everyone else."

"I have a headache." That was partially true. He rubbed his fingers over his temple in a vain attempt to ease the throbbing.

"Well, swallow some aspirin and get your shoes. You're coming to the fireworks display."

Nathan crossed his arms over his chest and simply stared. The withering look usually worked on Zach. He hoped it would have the same effect on her.

She crossed her arms, mirroring his stance, and waited.

He jerked his head toward the still-open door. "You might as well leave. I'm not going anywhere."

"Zach needs to see you attempting to live a normal life. How do you expect him to move on when you bury your head in the sand like this?" She marched into the room, picked up the plate with half an uneaten sandwich on it and jabbed it toward him. "Is this your dinner? That's pathetic when there are ribs and hamburgers outside."

His temper ignited. He strode toward her and yanked the plate from her fingers. "What I eat or don't eat is none of your business."

She snatched the remote and pressed the power button.

"I was watching that."

"Not anymore. Where are your shoes? And you might need a jacket if it gets cool later."

"I am not six years old—"

"Then start acting like it." She fisted her hands on her hips and glared at him.

Nathan opened his mouth, then clamped his lips together, unsure what might come out. Something unministerial, that's for sure.

"Look, Nathan. Almost all the parents are out there sharing the holiday with their children. What message are you sending Zach by staying in here?"

"That I don't like crowds?"

"Wrong. That you don't like *him*."

Her words reverberated off the walls around him, shaming him with their truth. All the resentment drained out of him, and he sagged onto the nearest chair. He did not deserve to be a parent. He couldn't function at all, not for himself, not even for Zach.

The warmth of a hand on his arm made him raise his head. "You can do this, Nathan. For Zach's sake. He needs to see you there, even if you only say two words to him. Just knowing you're there will mean everything to him."

The compassion swirling in the depth of her eyes mesmerized him. More than anything he needed a lifeline. Maybe Paige McFarlane could be his.

She took his hand and tugged him to his feet. "Come on. I'll walk down with you."

When all the kids were seated on the lawn and the fireworks had finally started, Paige made her way over to the picnic table where Nathan was sitting. Her heart swelled with sympathy. The poor guy looked as if he was at a funeral instead of a party. Still, he'd spent a few minutes with his son, before Zach and Peter had run off to join a game of hide-and-seek with the other campers. But Paige didn't miss the relief on Zach's face when he first saw his father.

She hopped up onto the table top to sit beside Nathan. "You doing okay?"

"Fine."

He didn't sound fine. Not one little bit. A thought hit Paige. Perhaps this holiday had special meaning for him and his wife. Why hadn't she thought of that before?

"Is this day bringing up sad memories?" she asked quietly.

Nathan stiffened beside her. "How did you know?"

"Not hard to figure out. Holidays, birthdays, anniversaries…they're all tough dates to get through." She clasped her hands on her lap. "I usually try to do something different to change the significance of the date." Like going rock climbing on the day she should have been married. "Hard to change Independence Day though." She gave him a smile, hoping to lighten his mood.

He shifted on the wooden surface to look at her. "So you lost someone close to you?"

She swallowed, then turned to meet his questioning gaze. "I did."

"A parent?"

She looked away, wishing she could deny God's gentle

nudging to share her grief. If her story could help Nathan in some small way, she had no choice but to share it. "No. My fiancé."

She felt him stiffen. "I'm so sorry. That must have been difficult."

The laugher of children drifted by them, a direct contradiction to the seriousness of their conversation.

"You have no idea." She gripped her fingers together, steeling herself for the onslaught of pain. "Colin was killed in a car accident—three weeks before our intended wedding day."

He sucked in a breath. "How awful. When did this happen?"

"Almost four years ago now. But sometimes it feels like yesterday." She blinked to keep any tears from forming. "At the time I believed Colin's accident was all my fault."

Nathan reached over and covered her hands with his own. She started at the warm strength of his fingers.

"What happened?" he asked quietly after several moments.

She hesitated, praying she could do this without falling apart. "I hadn't seen Colin in days. He'd been working on his thesis nonstop to finish before the wedding. I knew he was exhausted, but I was feeling sorry for myself, overwhelmed with wedding preparations. I begged him to come over." She drew in a ragged breath. "The police couldn't say for sure what happened, except they found his car wrapped around a telephone pole—with Colin dead at the scene."

A round of fireworks exploded in the air with a burst of color. Paige squeezed her eyes shut. Terrible visions of the past rose in her imagination. The flashing lights at the site of the accident when she arrived, the police officer's grim expression, the smell of the rain as it hit the pavement. With supreme effort, she dragged herself back to the present, to the feel of her hands captured in Nathan's strong, warm ones. She swallowed hard several times to push back the tears. "Like you with your wife, I blamed myself for his death. If I hadn't been so selfish, making him come out in the bad weather, he would still be alive. The guilt paralyzed me for months."

"How did you get past it?" Desperation laced his voice as tightly as his fingers squeezed her hand.

She focused her gaze on the small spray of dark hairs covering the back of his wrist. "My parents found me a wonderful therapist who saved my sanity. Gradually I realized the only way I could move forward was to forgive myself."

A starburst of red split the sky. "Were you really able to do that?" He sounded awestruck, as though she'd discovered a cure to the world's problems.

Paige took a breath. "For the most part. After a lot of therapy and a lot of prayer." She turned to look at him, and the anguish in Nathan's eyes struck a chord deep within her. She remembered that pain all too well—the remnants of it still haunted her. "I learned that you can't live your life with constant regret. Horrible things happen sometimes, and there's nothing we can do, except pray for the strength to get through them."

He released a long breath. "I'll have to take your word for it. Maybe someday I'll learn how to do that."

For a moment their gazes locked, fused by the common thread of pain they shared. A final burst of fireworks shook the night, followed by wild applause and whistling. Nathan cleared his throat and slowly removed his hand from hers.

The noise of the kids' hollers tore Paige's attention back to the present, and she hopped down from her perch. Zach, Peter and Kyle flew up the grass toward them, wild warlike whoops erupting from them. Maybe it was a result of sharing such an emotional story, but Paige's eyes stung with sudden tears at the sight of Zach laughing with the other boys.

He skidded to a halt in front of Nathan. "Hey, Dad. Weren't those fireworks cool?"

Nathan nodded. "Absolutely. I'm glad I came."

"I am, too. Maybe you can come watch our ball game tomorrow."

It was the opening Paige had prayed for. She held her breath, willing Nathan not to disappoint his son.

"I'd like that."

Zach smiled. "Awesome."

The sound of Jerry's whistle shrilled above the noise of the crowd.

"Gotta go. Night, Dad. See you tomorrow."

The threesome raced off toward Jerry, excitement radiating off them. Paige smiled to herself. They'd have a hard time getting the kids settled tonight after all the excitement. But it was worth it.

She turned to Nathan. "That's my cue. Thanks for coming out. I think it did Zach a world of good."

Nathan's lips tugged up in a half smile. "I know it did for me. Thanks for dragging me out of my cave."

Paige grinned. "Somebody had to poke the bear. I hope I won't have to get so pushy next time."

She went to leave, but he reached for her hand.

"Thank you for telling me about your fiancé. It helps to know I'm not alone—that someone else has experienced the same thing and survived."

Paige went still. "You're never alone, Nathan. God is always with you. He'll help you get through this, just like He helped me."

The next day, Paige carried her supper tray through the cafeteria, trying to ignore the pressure at her temples. Lack of sleep, as well as some cranky kids, had combined to make it a trying afternoon, the result of which was a tension headache that had only worsened as the day went on. She'd left Jerry and Sandy to supervise the cleanup of baseball equipment, while she went to scrounge some aspirin from Lou. Now she'd beat them to the cafeteria. She grabbed some utensils and crossed the floor. Her mood plummeted the moment she saw Brandon Marshall sprawled in a chair at her usual table.

He wore a cocky grin, watching her approach. "There you are, sugar."

"Hello, Brandon." She took a seat, scanning the room for Jerry or Sandy, wishing for an excuse to leave.

"Haven't seen you around much."

She focused on unfolding her napkin. "I've been busy with camp."

He leaned forward. "Well, that changes tonight. It's Friday and I'm taking you to a party in town."

Annoyance added to the throbbing in her skull, but she fought to keep her tone neutral. "Sorry, I can't. I'm heading up the campfire later."

Brandon snorted, his hair falling over his forehead. "You'd pass up a party for a lame sing-along?"

"It's my job."

"I'll get someone to cover for you."

Her fingers tightened on her fork. This game had grown immensely tedious. "I'm sorry, Brandon. I'm not interested in going out with you—or anyone else for that matter." She stabbed a fry with a bit more force than necessary.

Brandon straightened on his chair. "So let me get this straight. Because your last boyfriend kicked the bucket, you're never going to date again?"

Her fork clattered to the tabletop, his callous words striking like a physical blow. Seconds later, ripe anger rose in her chest. She clenched her trembling hands on the edge of the table. "I don't expect you to understand, but I lost the love of my life. I'm trying my best to get past it, in whatever way I can."

You'll have to be more forceful this time so he gets the message loud and clear. Sandy's words echoed in her head.

"The truth is, Brandon," she said firmly, "if I ever do decide to date again, it won't be with you."

He leaped to his feet, unleashed fury twisting his features. "I knew it. You think you're too good for me."

"You better believe she's too good for you, Marshall. Do yourself a favor and take no for an answer." An incensed Jerry approached the table, glaring daggers at Brandon.

Brandon snarled, focusing all his animosity at Jerry, who didn't move a muscle. Paige's heart pumped hard in her chest as she got to her feet, prepared to throw herself between the two if the situation escalated into violence. After several tense moments, Brandon stalked out of the room. The other employees, silently observing the stressful exchange, went back to their meals. Sandy stood in the doorway, holding back a group of kids trying to peer around her.

How much had they seen?

Paige sank back onto her chair.

Jerry placed a steadying hand on her shoulder. "You okay?"

"Yeah. Thanks for the save."

"No prob." He sat down beside her, an unusual scowl bunching his freckles together. "Better watch yourself, kid. Sandy may be right. That guy could be trouble."

Chapter Six

"Willy's eating the cat treats we brought him." Zach bounced into the stall where Paige was shoveling fresh straw.

"That's great." She blew loose strands of hair off her face, thankful that Zach had opted to spend his free time after dinner with her in the barn in order to check on the kitten rather than join in a quick game of horseshoes with the other kids. Paige hoped it meant he was beginning to trust her.

Zach tugged on her arm to get her attention. "Willy only eats the treats if I feed him."

She smiled down at his eager face. "That's because he likes you. You're his special person."

Zach grinned. "I guess I am."

Paige leaned on her pitchfork. "How'd you like to feed the horses for me while I finish here?"

His eyes lit with excitement and Paige marveled at the difference a week had made. The usual scowl showed up much less often now. He seemed relaxed and more open. Her mind circled back to Nathan and how much he'd missed of Zach's childhood. What kind of job did he have that required such long hours away from his family? And why was he so mysterious about it? She could probably ask Zach or George, but somehow that seemed like a violation of his privacy. She'd have to wait until Nathan felt ready to tell her.

Paige finished with the stall and stepped out into the corridor.

Zach reappeared, this time frowning. "Something's wrong with Mabel. She's not eating her food."

"I'll come and see." Paige clicked the door closed and followed him down to Mabel's stall.

"You're right," she agreed, after examining the mare. "She doesn't seem herself. I'll have the vet come out tomorrow and check on her." She tousled his hair affectionately. "You have a real knack with animals."

"Thanks. I think they know when people love them."

"They sure do." She paused, giving Mabel a final pat. "People sometimes aren't as smart as animals that way. They turn love into something very complicated. Like your dad, for instance."

Zach shot her a suspicious glance.

She picked up a bucket beside Mabel's water trough. "Remember when you told me he wouldn't forgive your mother?"

"Yeah." Zach followed her to the tap, where she began to fill the container.

She turned off the water and stopped to gauge Zach's reaction. He watched her, a slight frown on his face. "Your mother hurt your dad very badly when she left. His heart hadn't healed up enough to let her come home. He was afraid of getting hurt again."

His frown deepened. "My dad isn't afraid of anything."

"Everyone gets scared, Zach, even grown-ups. We just try not to show it."

Zach seemed lost in thought for a second or two. "My mom had a boyfriend, you know. I guess Dad was afraid she'd go back with him again."

Paige marveled at the insight of this seven-year-old. "Sometimes forgiveness takes time. But not letting your mom come back had nothing to do with you. Your father loves you very much."

She paused, half expecting an argument, but Zach only shrugged and bent to pick up the pail. Paige let out a sigh, thankful that the usual angry scowl hadn't reappeared. At least he was considering the possibility that his father loved him.

Paige sent up a quick prayer of gratitude. She would take every small victory she could get.

Nathan pushed back from the table in the Reynoldses' kitchen and patted his stomach. "Thank you, Catherine. That was a wonderful meal."

Catherine Reynolds turned, spatula in hand, and pushed a chestnut curl off her round forehead. "You haven't even had a second piece of pie."

Nathan groaned. "I'll have to waddle back to the inn as it is."

George chuckled and clapped him on the back. "Why don't we take Goliath for a walk and burn off some of those calories."

"Sounds good." A measure of relief slid through him. As much as he loved Catherine, her constant sympathetic glances were starting to grate on him.

Catherine plucked the pie off the table. "I'll wrap you up a piece to take back with you."

"Thanks for the dinner, honey." George kissed his wife on the cheek as he grabbed the leash from the hook on the wall. Seconds later, Goliath barreled into the room, tongue lolling.

Nathan shook his head. "How does he know?"

"Doggie radar." George grinned as he clipped on the leash and the two men stepped out into the refreshing air.

By mutual consent they walked in silence until they reached the path by the lake. From the corner of his eye,

Nathan could see George sliding him glances. "Something on your mind, George?"

George tugged on the leash to curb Goliath's enthusiasm. "I can't help but notice you seem…less tense than when you first got here. Is it the fresh air and good food, or is there another reason?"

Nathan frowned, not sure what his friend was getting at. "I think," he said slowly, "that seeing Zach relate to Paige, and to the other kids, has taken some of the weight off."

"And?"

"And what?" Nathan ignored the discomfort between his shoulder blades.

"How are *you* getting along with Paige? I hope your initial reservations about her have been resolved."

Nathan shoved his hands into his pockets and tried not to picture her big green eyes filled with tears as she relayed her tragic tale. "We're getting along fine."

"I'm glad."

They walked on in silence again.

"She told me about her fiancé," he said quietly.

George stopped dead on the path. "She did?"

Nathan nodded.

"Wow. That's big. She never talks about Colin."

"Did you know her when it happened?"

"Yeah, she was a mess. Had us real worried. We were all thankful when she found a way out of the grief and depression."

Nathan let out a slow breath. "Maybe, if I'm lucky, she can show me how to do the same. She's one strong lady, that's for sure."

George's eyes narrowed as he studied Nathan. "Paige is like a daughter to Catherine and me. She's been through more than most of us in her short life, and through it all, she's never lost her kindness or her innate optimism."

Nathan stilled. "Why are you telling me this?"

George's eyebrows crawled to the middle of his brow. "You're my friend, Nate. I love you like a son, but I don't think—"

Nathan's phone chimed in his pocket. He pulled it out and frowned at the unfamiliar number displayed. "Sorry, I'd better take this."

George gave a curt nod and stepped away, Goliath in tow.

Nathan clicked a button. "Nathan Porter."

"Reverend Porter, this is Bishop Telford."

Bands of tension tightened across the back of Nathan's neck. "Yes, sir. What can I do for you?"

"I'm calling to see if you've made a decision as to whether or not you'll be returning to your position at Saint Stephen's. Because if not, we need to start looking for your replacement."

The moon was full and high over the trees when Paige stepped out of the cabin. She breathed in the warm night air before setting off down the path. For some reason, she'd awoken at midnight and couldn't get back to sleep. After tossing and turning for close to an hour on the hard wooden bed—a sacrifice indeed compared with the luxurious mattress in her room at the inn—a change of scenery seemed in order. She pulled on a T-shirt and track pants and headed over to check on Mabel. The vet was scheduled to come by the next day, but if Mabel had taken a turn for the worse, Paige would put in an emergency call.

As she strolled past the pit where they'd held the campfire a few hours earlier, she smiled to herself. Tonight's sing-along had been a roaring success. Paige had been surprised to see Nathan join the group. It wasn't unusual for some of the adults to participate, but somehow Paige didn't picture Nathan as the campfire type. She caught him watching her more than once as she and Jerry played their guitars, leading the group in song. His gaze had unnerved her, made her heart beat faster. Despite her discomfort, she'd been glad to see him sitting behind Zach. Close enough for Zach to be aware of his presence, but not enough to interfere with his friends.

Paige shivered slightly as she made her way into the stable. When she flipped the switch, the overhead light cast a dim glow down the main corridor. The horses whinnied softly in welcome. She took a moment to greet each one and reassure them that her late-night visit was not cause for alarm. Yet the animals' unease vibrated in the air. Maybe they sensed Mabel's illness.

"Hey, girl," she crooned, noting the mare's full feedbag. "You're not yourself today, are you? Doc Miller's coming tomorrow and he'll fix you right up."

Paige stroked Mabel's brown nose, hoping to impart a soothing touch. Or maybe she was trying to ease her own anxiety. Tonight the shadows seemed ominous, the wind malevolent. She jumped a moment later when the creak of the main door echoed through the building. A ripple of unease raced up her spine. Had the wind blown it open or had someone come in?

Her question was answered when the unmistakable thud of footsteps rang out.

Struggling to control her fear, Paige searched for a possible weapon. "Who's there?"

A figure stepped out of the shadows and she jumped back in alarm. "Brandon." Her hand flew to her chest. "You scared me. What are you doing here?"

"I just got back and saw you come in here. I wanted to tell you about the great party you missed." His eyes glittered in the dim light. Paige's uneasiness grew at the slur of his words and his staggered gait.

"I was checking on the horses, but I'd better get back now." She tucked her trembling hands into her pockets and started to move past him, only to recoil when he snagged her by the arm.

"Not so fast, Miss Goody Two-shoes. I'm not finished with you yet."

The stench of stale cigarette smoke and beer assaulted her as she fought to keep down the panic rising within her. She tugged at his viselike grip on her arm. "Let go of me."

Instead, Brandon tightened his fingers and dragged her along the corridor until they reached an empty stall. Paige dug her feet into the floor, using all her weight to fight his momentum. When he shoved her through the stall door, she stumbled, scraping her knees as she hit the floor. She sucked in a breath against the pain.

Ruthlessly, he dragged her back to her feet, his eyes glassy. "Now we'll continue the party right here." He leered at her, pulling her closer. "I hope you've been saving your kisses for me."

Paige pushed her hands against his chest and opened her mouth to scream. Instead, hot lips clamped down hard over hers, filling her mouth with the bitter taste of alcohol. Fear and anger pumped her with adrenaline as she struggled wildly to free herself. For someone so wiry, Brandon had amazing strength. Her efforts proved futile against him. Wrenching a hand free, she raked her nails down his cheek.

Like an angry bull, he bellowed in surprise and momentarily loosened his grip. Paige seized the opportunity to thrust herself away from him.

"You little—"

Brandon's fist shot out and struck her hard across the face. The force of the blow sent her reeling backward into the straw. He was on top of her before she could move, his face twisted into an ugly mask. Paige tried to push herself up, but he knocked her back. Her ears rang from the blow to her head. The metallic taste of blood filled her mouth, and tears stung her eyes as the terrible knowledge of what was about to happen hit home.

Help me, Lord.

With one final heroic effort, she opened her mouth and screamed.

Chapter Seven

Nathan kicked off the tangled sheets and pushed out of bed. No matter which way he turned, sleep eluded him. Too many unwelcome thoughts filled his head. Thoughts of the past...and thoughts of Paige.

Lately, Nathan found himself contemplating the complexities of this unique woman all too often. The fact that she'd suffered such a terrible tragedy and went on to overcome her despair and guilt had earned Nathan's admiration. But Paige McFarlane could not be his savior. He had to do the work to resolve his own emotional issues.

Nathan donned his jeans and a T-shirt, throwing on his Windbreaker in case there was a breeze by the water. A brisk walk in the fresh air would do him good.

He'd come to the point where the path veered off to the woods when he heard the scream. The terror and intensity of it tore through him. His pulse rate spiked as he set off at a jog in the direction of the stables. When he neared the barn, a second bloodcurdling shriek erupted.

"Paige."

He had no time to wonder how he knew it was her before charging into the building.

It took a moment for his eyes to adjust to the lighting, but he forged ahead, calling her name. A flurry of movement from one of the stalls caught his attention. Nathan burst into the enclosure and paused only a second to take in the scene before him. Two people struggled fiercely in the straw on the floor—fists and legs flailing. Then he saw Paige's bloody face contorted with anguish, her blond hair spread in disarray over the straw.

A type of rage unknown to him raced through his veins, igniting like wildfire over dry tinder. With a roar, he yanked the man up by the back of his shirt and threw him out into the corridor. The man slammed into the wall and slid to the ground. Seconds later, he scrambled to his feet and charged at Nathan. Fueled by adrenaline, Nathan was more than ready for him. He ducked the man's attack and plowed his fist into the guy's face, knocking him out cold.

Nathan quickly bound the lowlife's hands and feet with some rope so he couldn't get up again, and then returned to the stall, where he found Paige curled into a fetal position, a fall of hair curtaining her face. Another burst of anger surged through him at the sight of her torn clothing. He prayed to God he'd been in time, but pushed the thought away and focused on regaining his composure. Paige needed calm reassurance, not fury.

Nathan knelt beside her in the straw and placed a tentative hand on her arm, but she flinched away from him.

"It's okay. You're safe now." Gently he pushed the hair back from her face.

His pulse stalled at the sight of blood running from the side of her mouth and a large purple welt forming on her cheek. He pulled off his Windbreaker, wrapped it around her and gathered her into his arms. Her slight form shook as she buried her face into his shoulder, one hand clutching his shirt.

"I'm taking you to the inn. We'll call the police from there."

In her state of shock, he wondered if she'd even heard him.

Minutes later, he pushed into the darkened kitchen and

snapped on a light. Paige burrowed deeper into his chest to avoid the brightness. He strode past the long steel prep area, found a chair and sat down with her on his lap.

The hot tears that soaked his shirtfront seemed to melt straight through the ice surrounding his heart. As he absorbed her tremors, a long-forgotten tenderness overwhelmed him. With one hand stroking her hair, he murmured words of comfort. For a moment, the world consisted of nothing but his steady breathing and their shared body warmth. After several long minutes, when the shaking subsided, he reluctantly moved her off his lap to another chair.

"I'll get some ice for your face," he said. "Be right back."

On his way to the large freezer at the far end of the long kitchen, he made a quick phone call to George from his cell phone, explaining the situation. In a fury-checked voice, George promised to call the police before heading right over.

Ice pack in hand, Nathan returned to Paige. He sat beside her and placed it gently on her bruised cheek. She reached up to hold the pack in place, staring at him with haunted eyes.

"Are you hurt anywhere else?" he asked gently.

"I–I don't think so."

She sat swamped in his Windbreaker, like a lost waif. Her bare legs, visible through large, ragged tears in her pants, were streaked with blood.

"Did he…he didn't…?" Nathan couldn't get the words out.

She shook her head as fresh tears gathered in her eyes.

"Thank God." Relief loosened his muscles. Physical wounds would heal, but the effects of a rape would last forever.

She brushed at the dampness on her unmarred cheek. "How did you find me, anyway?"

"I was out for a walk and heard you scream." He shifted on his chair. "What were you doing out so late?"

"I couldn't sleep, so I went to check on one of the horses. Brandon saw me go into the stables." She shivered.

"You know him then?"

She nodded. "He works here. He invited me to a party earlier, but I turned him down. He came back drunk and angry."

"A dangerous combination." Nathan banked down the rage that simmered under his skin.

She sucked in a breath. "How can I ever thank you?" she whispered. "If you hadn't been there…"

"Try not to think about that. You're safe, and Brandon will be the police's problem very shortly."

"You called the police?" A note of panic rang in her voice.

"I called George and he called the police. They should both be here any minute."

Her stricken eyes darted to the door as if expecting a monster.

"We had to call the authorities," he said. "Brandon committed a crime. He can't be allowed to get away with it." He moved on his chair, his knee brushing hers. "I'll be right here with you. So will George. He and Catherine are going to take you back to their house tonight."

She plucked at a loose thread on her torn pants. "I'm sorry," she said. "The thought of talking to the police is bringing back bad memories for me."

He should have realized. "Your fiancé's accident?"

She nodded.

Not knowing what else to say, he reached over to lift the ice pack from her frozen fingers. The swelling on her face had subsided, but a nasty, purple bruise marred her pale skin.

The sound of footsteps in the hall alerted them to the arrival of George and Catherine, along with two police officers. Catherine rushed straight over to Paige and threw her arms around her, causing a fresh wave of tears from Paige.

Nathan thanked God for Catherine's nurturing spirit as she offered Paige a type of comfort that he could not.

"There now. Don't you worry about a thing," she said to Paige. "After you talk with the sergeant here, I'm going to get you a nice, hot bath and a cup of tea."

George hovered in the doorway, arms crossed across his barrel chest. Nathan could tell by his scowl he was seething inside.

"The guy's unconscious in the barn," Nathan told the officer. He wondered if they would ask how he got that way, but they didn't.

One man nodded, then sent his partner out to look after Brandon. "I'd like to speak with Miss McFarlane now." He pulled out a pen and notebook from his pocket.

Nathan stepped toward the man and lowered his voice. "She's been through a lot tonight. I trust you'll be considerate of that fact."

George put a restraining hand on his shoulder. "Of course he will, Nate. Let Sergeant Williams do his job."

"Fine, but I'm staying here while he questions her."

Nathan was not about to let Paige be upset or bullied by anyone else tonight.

The sun was high in the sky when Paige awoke the next day. She groaned and burrowed under the warmth of the blankets, grateful George had given her the day off to recuperate. Her body ached all over. The expression "hit by a truck" came to mind more than once.

The guest room in George and Catherine's house was as beautiful as one of the suites at the inn. Yet sleep had eluded her for most of the night. Every time she dozed off, nightmares of the assault plagued her. Finally, somewhere near dawn, exhaustion took over and she fell into a deep, dreamless sleep.

Now, as she slowly stretched her sore muscles, her thoughts turned to Nathan. The comfort she'd found in his protective embrace had surprised her, as did her reluctance to let him go. He'd stood by her the entire time she answered the police's questions, finally sending the officers away when he felt she'd had enough. His sensitivity surprised her more than a little.

The bedroom door opened and Catherine's head poked around the corner. "Oh good, you're awake." She pushed into the room, balancing a breakfast tray. "I made you some French toast and bacon. A good meal will help you feel better."

Without waiting for a reply, she settled the tray over Paige's legs. Fresh orange juice and coffee rounded out the feast.

Paige breathed in the enticing aroma of the food, wishing she had an appetite. "This looks wonderful. Thank you."

"You're more than welcome." Catherine pulled up a chair. "How are you feeling today?"

"Banged up and a little shaky."

Catherine patted her hand. "That's normal after a scare like that. It'll take some time to forget."

Paige nodded as she sampled a bite of the French toast to please Catherine.

"George wanted me to let you know Brandon won't be coming back. He fired him on the spot."

Relief flooded Paige's aching muscles. "I'm glad." She sighed. "I never imagined he would hurt me. It seemed like an annoying but harmless crush."

"Well, that's all over now." Catherine smoothed her skirt as she rose. "I'll let you eat in peace. By the way, you have some visitors waiting in the kitchen. Do you feel up to it?"

She nodded, her mouth full. "Give me a minute to finish and I'll come out."

"Take your time, honey. They aren't going anywhere."

Nathan sat in the Reynoldses' big, homey kitchen, sipping coffee. Funny how this room hadn't changed since he'd been coming here as a kid. The same wooden cupboards, the same oak table and the same lace curtains at the windows. The enticing aroma of fresh coffee and muffins. Nathan remembered feeling very safe and happy here, which probably explained his relaxed attitude now as he watched his son playing with Goliath. Zach laughed with delight as Goliath wet his entire face with one tongue lap.

"Easy, boy. I'm not a popsicle." He wiped his cheeks with mock disgust, but the big dog only cocked his head, waiting for the expected treat.

Nathan hoped Paige wouldn't mind him bringing Zach to see her. Apparently from what George told him, when Paige didn't appear at breakfast that morning, the kids had been full of questions, which George had handled as best he could. Jerry and Sandy planned to bring the rest of the kids by later. But to alleviate Zach's fear for Paige's well-being, Nathan had given in to his badgering and allowed him to come over first thing. Nathan understood that after losing his mother in such a shocking manner, Zach needed to see Paige for himself, bruises and all.

Catherine entered the kitchen, a laundry basket hitched on a plump hip. "Paige will be out in a few minutes," she said, setting the load down.

Zach scrambled up to the table and grabbed a crayon to put the finishing touches on the get-well card he'd made. When the sound of a door opening caught his attention, Zach snatched the page and raced down the hallway.

Catherine smiled as she folded a towel. "Zach is certainly taken with Paige. She's done wonders with him in such a short amount of time."

Nathan set down his mug and pushed up from the table. "The true test will be when we go home."

Catherine stopped folding, walked over and enveloped Nathan in a fierce hug. "Give it some time, honey. I promise things will get better."

His throat tightened at her simple, loving gesture. He swallowed and kissed her cheek. "Thank you, Catherine."

"You're welcome." She plucked the basket off the table. "Now, I'll let you have some time alone." She gave him a wink and disappeared down the hall.

Before Nathan could collect his emotions, Paige hobbled into the kitchen beside Zach, his colorful card in hand. She was dressed in a long pink bathrobe, and her pale hair hung loose over her shoulders, partly obscuring the bruises on her face.

"I can't believe you drew this all by yourself," she said to Zach. "It's beautiful. Thank you." She ruffled the curls on Zach's head.

He beamed with pleasure at the compliment, then his smile faded. "I'm sorry you got hurt, Paige."

"Me, too." She looked up then, and her eyes met Nathan's. "I'm just thankful your dad was there to rescue me."

Nathan shoved his hands in his pockets as a swath of heat moved up his neck.

Zach scrunched his nose. "So Dad's kind of a hero?"

Her steady gaze stayed on Nathan. "Yes, he is."

Nathan squirmed in his loafers, about to deny her assertion, when Zach looked at Nathan and smiled. Nathan's heart swelled at the admiration on his son's face. It had been so long since Zach had looked up to him, Nathan had forgotten how good it felt. The appreciation in Paige's eyes didn't hurt either.

He pulled out a chair for Paige. "You look a little wobbly. Better sit down."

She nodded, wincing as she lowered herself stiffly to the seat.

"Sore?"

"Like a horse kicked me."

Nathan reached out a finger to gently brush her hair aside, frowning at the swelling on her cheek. "You need some more ice." He opened Catherine's freezer and pulled out a tray. Deftly, he dumped the cubes into a soft dish towel.

Zach squirmed beside Paige's chair, tugging her arm to get her attention. "I wish you could come with us today. We're going on a nature hike in the woods to look for fossils. I'm gonna find a dinosaur bone."

"That sounds amazing." Paige looked as if she actually believed him.

Zach grinned. "I'd better go. I don't want everyone to leave without me."

"I'll be right there to walk you over," Nathan said. "I need to talk to Paige for a minute."

"'Kay, Dad." Zach unhooked Goliath's leash from the back door and, with a wave, followed the eager dog outside, letting the screen door slam behind him.

Nathan sat down beside Paige and handed her the makeshift icepack. "I went with George to the courthouse earlier. Brandon has been released on bail into his parents' custody, pending a court date."

A slight frown wrinkled her brow. "You didn't have to do that."

He shifted his weight on the hard chair. "I wanted to make sure he wouldn't bother you again. And you don't have to worry about him coming back here. George is having his things shipped home."

The relief was evident on her face. "That's good to know. Thank you."

"You're welcome." He paused. "For what it's worth, he did seem sorry for what he did."

She didn't respond. Instead she fiddled with the long end of the robe's belt. Something in her demeanor sent off little flares of suspicion inside him.

He reached over to still her fidgeting fingers. "You know none of this was your fault, right?"

She sighed. "I know. Just second-guessing my actions, I guess."

"Well, don't." His tone was a little harsher than he'd intended. He paused to soften his voice. "Nothing you said or did could ever warrant his behavior. There's no excuse for violence."

Paige nodded, then looked at him with large solemn eyes that did crazy things to his pulse. "Thanks again for coming to my rescue."

"No thanks needed." He became aware he was still holding one of her hands. Clearing his throat, he released it and stood up. "I'd better not keep Zach waiting. If he feeds that dog any more treats, Catherine will have my head."

Her soft laugh warmed his insides.

"Keep that ice on for a while."

"I will."

With one last look at her, he exited through the back door and closed it behind him with a quiet click. He stood very still on the stoop, reeling from the sense that his world had unexpectedly shifted. Maybe it had to do with the way she looked at him, as if he was a hero. Or maybe it was just Paige herself, constantly surprising him with the strength she showed through every trial. Whatever the cause, for the first time in a long while, the hard space around his heart had softened enough to allow a certain woman past his defenses.

Zach ran up, Goliath on his heels. "Come on, Dad. Let's go."

Nathan nodded and rubbed the ache in his chest, remembering that keeping his emotions locked away was a much safer option.

He had a feeling he'd be reminding himself of that a lot in the weeks to come.

Chapter Eight

Paige stepped out of the Pine Ridge Community Church on Sunday morning and sent a silent prayer of thanks Heavenward that she was recovered enough to attend service this morning. Her spirits had lifted the moment she entered the white clapboard church.

Paige especially enjoyed listening to Pastor Dan Redding's sermons, which always challenged and uplifted her. The vibrant young minister brought a sense of exuberance to his services, and in the five years since he'd taken over in Pine Ridge, the congregation had almost doubled.

Dan stood at the bottom of the church steps, his boyish face beaming at each member he spoke to. While Sandy and Jerry herded the children toward the bus, Paige waited to speak with Dan. She needed to confirm her solo for next Sunday.

"Paige." He kissed her warmly on her good cheek, concern shadowing his eyes. "I was sorry to hear about your ordeal. How are you feeling?"

Paige forgot how quickly word of mouth spread in this rural area. "Much better, thank you. Where is Gwen today?" Paige usually looked forward to chatting with Dan's wife after the service.

The minister rolled his eyes in mock exasperation. "Johnny had an upset stomach. If one boy's not sick, the other one is."

Paige laughed. "Poor Gwen. Give her my love when you get home."

"I will. She'll be glad I saw you. She was worried after hearing about the assault."

Paige repressed a shudder. Just the word brought back a rush of horrible memories. She fiddled with her hair to make sure it covered her bruised cheek. "Tell her I'm fine."

"So you'll be able to sing with the choir next week as planned?"

"Wouldn't miss it."

"Great. We'll see you then."

On the bus ride back to Wyndermere, Paige watched Zach laughing with the other kids, and a spurt of disappointment washed over her as her thoughts turned to Nathan. She'd hoped he would join them for church this morning, for Zach's sake if nothing else. But though she'd waited in the lobby until the last possible minute, Nathan hadn't shown up.

Paige straightened on the hard bench seat as a sudden idea struck her. Dan Redding counseled his parishioners on many aspects of life, from marriage problems to bereavement. Perhaps Dan could help Nathan in a way that she couldn't. Man-to-man.

The more she thought about it over the course of the day, the more convinced she became. By the time dinner hour rolled around, Paige resolved to talk to Nathan. She made her excuses to Jerry and Sandy, changed into a simple yellow dress and set off for the main dining room at the inn.

Walking through the ornate Wyndermere lobby always gave Paige a secret thrill. The plush furniture, marble fireplace and exquisite crystal chandelier made her feel like a princess surveying her castle.

She caught her reflection in the mirrored foyer and paused. The light jacket she wore over her dress masked the injuries on her arms, but nothing could fully disguise her discolored cheek. She arranged her hair to cover it a bit better and continued on to the formal dining room. Stepping into the entrance, she glanced out over all the attractively clad guests and gripped her hands together. How would she broach her idea to Nathan without upsetting him?

"Good evening, Miss McFarlane. What can I do for you?" Henry, the manager of the dining room, stood at the reception desk.

"I'm looking for Mr. Porter. Is he here?"

"As a matter of fact, he is. In the far corner."

Paige scanned the room and spotted Nathan seated alone at a small table for two by the window overlooking the lake. He must've requested his own table. The resort usually tried to seat single guests together so they'd get to know each other.

"Will you be staying for dinner?" Henry asked.

"I'm not sure. I'll have to play that one by ear."

Now that she was here, her optimism gave way to uncertainty. What kind of reaction would her suggestion receive? She hoped their tentative friendship wouldn't revert to his previous hostility, but it was a risk she'd have to take.

Putting on her best smile, she crossed the elegant room, greeting staff and guests as she passed. With his back to her, Nathan didn't see her until she stood right in front of him.

"Hello, Nathan. May I speak to you for a minute?"

His head jerked up. "Paige. Yes, of course." Manners had him rising from his seat. "Is anything wrong?"

She shook her head. "Everything's fine."

Relief washed over his features. He rounded the table to pull out a chair for her. "Please sit down. Have you eaten?"

She remained standing, not wanting to appear as if she'd invited herself to a meal with him. "Not yet. I wanted to talk to you first."

"Why don't you join me and we can talk while we eat? I've just ordered."

She hesitated. Eating together in this setting felt too much like a date.

"Please stay. I could use the company." He flashed a rare smile that literally took her breath away. The sound of clinking cutlery and muted conversation faded into the background. She was aware only of his eyes on hers and his hand at her back.

"In that case, sure."

Nathan helped her with her chair, then signaled to one of the waiters, who came to take her order.

"This certainly beats the staff cafeteria," Paige said when he sat down.

"Your coworkers will be jealous." His voice held a hint of laughter as he took a sip of his iced tea.

"Yes, they will." She unrolled her utensils from the linen napkin. In the center of the table, a slim vase held a single pink rose and a small candle flickered in its glass holder. Paige swallowed, feeling more and more as if she was on a date. She looked up to see Nathan watching her, a question in his eyes. How did she bring up the topic of Dan Redding?

"Zach enjoyed the church service this morning." She attempted to sound casual. "I thought you might've come with him."

A nerve ticked in the tight line of his jaw. "I haven't been to church in some time now."

She was glad to know that at some point he'd had faith in God.

"I understand." She fingered her glass of water, tracing patterns in the condensation forming on the side. "After Colin's death, I found it hard to go back to church, too. I was angry with God as well as myself. Eventually, my minister helped me to accept forgiveness on a spiritual level."

The waiter arrived at that moment with their meals, two plates of prime rib and roasted vegetables.

"Why are you telling me this?" Nathan asked quietly.

Steam rose from the meal in front of her. She took a breath and plunged on. "I was hoping you'd come with us next Sunday. For one thing, I could use an adult to sit with the children since I'll be filling in for the soloist." She smoothed her napkin onto her lap.

"What's the real reason, Paige?"

She froze. Could he really see through her like that? Pinned by his gaze, her pulse hammered in her throat. "I want you to meet the pastor," she admitted. "He and his wife are good friends of mine. His name is Dan Redding. He's about your age, married with two boys…and very experienced with counseling of all types."

A confused frown wrinkled his brow. "Are you trying to tell me you want this pastor to take over with Zach?"

"No, no. Zach and I are doing fine."

"Then I don't understand." Exasperation tinged his words.

"I'm sorry. I've explained this all wrong." She paused, trying to gather her thoughts, which seemed to be ping-ponging around in her head. Lately, being around Nathan made her lose her normal composure. "I thought *you* might benefit from talking with Dan. From a professional standpoint, I think it's crucial that you deal with your own grief while Zach is dealing with his. Otherwise when you go home, you'll end up sabotaging the progress he's made."

He was silent for so long, she wasn't sure what to make of it. Had she offended him? She dabbed a bead of perspiration off her lip with a napkin.

"I don't need counseling," he said at last, his voice flat.

"Of course you do," she bristled. "The woman you loved just died in a most tragic manner. Believe me, I know what that's like."

Nathan dragged his hands through his hair, marring its usual immaculate condition. "That's just it. I didn't love her."

Paige's mouth fell open. "I don't understand."

Pushing his plate aside, he sighed. "I loved Cynthia when I married her. But that changed the day I found out she'd been cheating on me for almost a year." His brows drew together, forming a dark line.

Paige winced, trying to imagine a similar situation with Colin, certain the pain of such a betrayal would have been far worse than losing him through death.

"Don't get me wrong," Nathan added quickly. "Cynthia's death saddened me greatly, most of all because Zach will have to grow up without her. For all her faults, she was a devoted mother."

A wave of sympathy swamped Paige. "Don't you see, Nathan? You started grieving the minute she walked out on you, and you haven't stopped. In my professional opinion, you're stuck in the anger stage and can't move forward. You need help to do that."

His eyes narrowed and his jaw tightened.

"Do me a favor. Come next Sunday and meet Dan. See what you think of him before you make a decision."

His long fingers fiddled with his fork as he considered her words. "I'll think about it. That's all I can promise."

"Thank you." Relief loosened the air in her lungs and she could breathe again.

She'd managed to get her idea across without damaging their fragile friendship. And no matter what happened with Dan, getting Nathan back to church would be a good thing.

She'd leave the rest up to God.

On Tuesday afternoon, while the kids were busy with Sandy and Jerry on the beach, Paige paced in front of the barn, staring at the closed door, and huffed out an annoyed breath.

"You're being ridiculous," she muttered to herself.

It was a beautiful sunny afternoon. What better time to go back and face the place of her attack? Nothing scary about checking on the horses in broad daylight. She wiped her palms on the side of her shorts.

After a lengthy internal debate, she used an old piece of wood to prop the door wide open, and mustering what was left of her courage, she marched into the main corridor toward Mabel's stall. Very little light penetrated the dim building. Her steps slowed at the sound of the horses' soft whinnies and Horatio's hooves stamping out a welcome. Everything was as it should be—very normal.

In the end, the smell undid her. The musty aroma of straw mixed with strong animal scents brought the terror of that night flooding back. Her body trembled as the icy claws of panic gripped her. Turning, she raced out the main door and kept running until she reached one of the cabins. There she stopped and leaned against the wood railing, eyes closed, her breath coming in heaving gasps. Disgusted at her cowardice, she sank onto one of the steps and dropped her head into her hands.

"Hard to go back?"

The masculine voice had her heart hammering before she looked up. Nathan stood a few feet away, looking very fit in tan shorts and a crisp white T-shirt.

Why did his neatness always make her feel so disheveled?

"Harder than I thought." She swiped her forearm across her damp brow. "It's infuriating. I have to be able to go in there to look after the animals without freaking out every time."

He stepped toward her and held out a hand. "Maybe some company would help."

She stared into his reassuring face and knew she would always feel safe with him. Slowly, she placed her palm in his, and he helped her to her feet. With her hand firmly tucked in his, they walked back to the barn, where he paused outside the dark opening.

"Let me know if you want to leave at any time."

She nodded and together they entered the open door. It wasn't as bad the second time, now that she was prepared for the sounds and smells to assault her. The anxiety welled up again, but this time she allowed it to roll over her, taking several deep breaths to get through it.

Nathan kept a strong grip on her hand as they moved forward. From the corner of her eye, she saw Mabel toss her head and snort, as if indignant that Paige was ignoring her. Paige's attention, however, remained focused on one particular stall. She knew she had to face the location of her attack.

"Are you sure you're up to this?" Nathan moved beside her.

"Not really, but it's something I have to do."

As if by unspoken agreement, he opened the stall door and waited for her to make the next move. Slowly she stepped inside and let the atmosphere sweep over her. The area had been tidied up—the straw removed, the floor swept clean. All traces of blood and violence had, thankfully, been eradicated.

Nathan seemed to sense her need for silence. He stood waiting while she walked slowly around the enclosure, then turned back to face him, hugging her arms across her midsection.

"Nothing here can hurt me." She was annoyed to find her knees still shaky.

He nodded. "Fear can only have the power you give it."

Stepping back over the threshold, she lifted her chin. "Then I choose to give it none."

When Nathan drew her into his arms, she didn't resist. Once again she found comfort and security there, inhaling the now-familiar scent of him. Finally, because she knew she must, she drew away. "I should feed the horses."

"I'll come with you."

Grateful for his calming presence, she nodded. Nathan followed her to each stall while she filled the feedbags and put out fresh water. She gave Mabel an extra pat, glad to see the vet had cured her digestive issues. When she finished, they left the barn together and she secured the main door.

Sliding her hands into her pockets, she blew out a long breath that lifted her bangs. "Thanks. I don't know if I could've faced that alone."

"It should get easier each time you go back. Maybe you could have the kids help you in the meantime." He smiled, then cocked his head. "I was about to go for a jog. Care to join me?"

In her present vulnerable state, Paige shouldn't risk the temptation of spending more time with him, but how could she refuse when he'd been so kind? She eyed him skeptically. "Make that a walk and you're on."

Amusement spread across his handsome features. "A walk it is."

They entered the woods and hiked side by side along an obscure path. The cool serenity of the treed area always eased Nathan's tension. He hoped it would do the same for Paige.

"How do you know your way around these woods so well?" Paige asked.

Nathan glanced over at her. "Part of my daily run cuts through here. The shade keeps the heat bearable."

"So you run every day?"

"I try to. It's a much nicer experience here than in the city. No smog or car fumes."

"It *is* beautiful here." She smiled. "That's a big part of why I keep coming back."

Nathan ducked under a low-hanging branch, holding it out of the way for her. "And where is home for you?" He found himself wanting to learn everything he could about her.

"Portsmouth, New Jersey. Near Atlantic City. But I'm attending college in New York right now." She reached down to pluck a flower from beside the path.

Nathan fell in step beside her. The pungent smell of pine and wildflowers drifted around them. "What will you do after you finish?"

"I want to start a grief-counseling program somewhere. Possibly through our local funeral home, affiliated with my church."

"So you'll be going back to New Jersey then." A wave of disappointment slid through him, but he pushed it away. Her future had nothing to do with him.

"That's the tentative plan. I know my parents are counting on it."

"You must miss your family."

"Very much. I'm going home for a few days next month. Mom is planning a big party for my brother Matt's twenty-first birthday." She tucked her hair behind one ear. By now, her bruises were barely noticeable.

They came out of the woods onto a path by the lake. Nathan led her to a wooden bench facing the water, where they sat down to rest for a moment.

She slid a glance at him. "What about you? Are you close with your parents?"

"Very close. Probably because I'm an only child."

"I'll bet you were horribly spoiled," she teased.

A smile tugged at the corner of his mouth. "Maybe a little."

A soft breeze came up, blowing Paige's hair around her face. Nathan reached over and pulled a strand away from her cheek. The scent of her light perfume filled his senses. Did she have any idea how beautiful she was? Almost against his will, his gaze fell to her mouth, her full lips slightly parted. He knew it was madness, but he couldn't seem to stop himself. All he could think of was kissing her.

His mouth was a whisper away from hers when she pulled back and jerked to her feet.

"I'm sorry...I should get going."

Nathan rose as well, disappointment and remorse crashing through him in equal measure. "I'll walk you back," he said quietly.

She nodded, and they started along the path in silence, her flushed cheeks giving away her discomfort.

He shoved his hands deep into his pockets, giving himself a mental slap.

Nice going, Porter. Only an idiot would almost kiss a woman when she was getting over an assault.

He needed to get a grip on his emotions and remember that neither one of them was ready for a romantic relationship. The sooner he got that through his thick head, the better off he'd be.

The crickets and bullfrogs joined efforts to produce a harmonious serenade, but its beauty was lost on Paige. Her mind was preoccupied with Nathan Porter and the terrifying feelings he'd begun to evoke in her.

When had she started to develop romantic interest in Nathan Porter?

A few weeks ago, she barely tolerated the man, and today they'd almost kissed. How had things turned upside down so quickly?

She sighed. Perhaps being rescued by Nathan had made her see him in a romantic light, like some type of story-book hero. Which meant her feelings must be based on fantasy, not reality.

Paige reached her favorite spot by the lake, took off her sandals and waded into the warm, shallow water. There was something soothing about the gentle play of the water over her bare feet, and the sensation of sand squishing between her toes.

Colin used to love the beach back home, especially on days when the ocean was rough and the waves crashed onto the rocks. Pain gripped her heart as she allowed memories buried in her subconscious to resurface once more. Memories of happy times shared with her fun-loving, free-spirited Colin. She remembered them frolicking in the waves, riding Rollerblades in the park and biking on the trails at home. And she recalled with vivid clarity the night he proposed in their favorite restaurant. That had been the happiest day of her life, full of dreams for the future. Dreams that had died along with Colin.

Long-repressed grief rose to the surface. She wrapped her arms around her middle like a shield and allowed the tears to slide unchecked down her cheeks.

Remember Colin lying in that casket. Remember the agony when they lowered him into the ground. That's what comes from loving too deeply.

She forced herself to relive the suffering, even briefly, as a reminder of why she would never subject herself to such pain again. Why she'd vowed never to love anyone that much, or give someone the power to hurt her.

With the back of her hand, she swiped the tears from her face. Fresh determination filled her senses as she walked back up the beach, sandals in hand. These feelings for Nathan were nothing more than misguided gratitude. Soon

Nathan and Zach would return to their lives in New York, and she would go back to school to finish her degree.

In the meantime, for her own sanity, she needed to avoid Nathan as much as possible.

Chapter Nine

Nathan straightened his tie, then looked at himself in the mirror. From the outside, he appeared calm and professional in his navy suit and crisp white shirt. Inside, he was a mass of conflicting emotions.

How had he let himself get talked into this? Was he really ready to step back into God's house for the first time in months? He released a long sigh. The only thing he knew for sure was that he couldn't let Paige down. So he would go to church with her this once, meet the pastor, then tell Paige that he didn't want—or need—counseling.

Especially not by a fellow minister.

His resolve set, he headed to the lobby and went out to meet the other churchgoers waiting for the bus. The sight of Paige looking fresh and pretty in a light green summer dress, her fair hair framing her face, had Nathan's heart knocking like the noisy bus engine. He couldn't help but recall their intimate moment by the lake the other day with a mixture of regret and relief. He had a feeling if they had shared that kiss, everything would've changed between them in ways neither of them was ready for.

Paige looked over and gave him a tentative smile as he approached the group. "You've decided to join us."

"For today. We'll see how it goes from there." He gave a quick nod, and boarded the bus before he could change his mind.

Half an hour later, seated in the front pew of Pine Ridge Community Church, Nathan tried to ignore the bead of sweat trickling down his back. Beside him, Zach sat straight and tall, his hymnbook open in readiness for the opening song. A bittersweet pang of pride surged in Nathan's chest. It had been a very long time since he'd looked out over his congregation to see Cynthia and Zach in the front row, offering their love and support of his ministry. At least, he'd thought Cynthia had supported his career. Too bad he'd been horribly mistaken.

Nathan turned and glanced over his shoulder at the parishioners behind him. How odd to be on this side of the altar, to be an anonymous member of a congregation, instead of leading the service. A sharp spasm of regret shot through him. He'd missed this sense of community. Without it, he felt isolated and lonely, like a ship without a port.

His gaze swung back to the empty pulpit awaiting the preacher. Unwelcome memories of his last sermon at Saint Stephen's rushed through him. The way he'd stopped midsentence, unable to continue, and simply stared out at the sea of puzzled faces. The way the cold, slick sweat had coated his entire body until panic had enveloped him and he'd fled, leaving his flock unattended. Abandoned.

The organ started, abruptly riveting his attention back to the choir and to Paige, standing tall in her red choir gown. Light from the stained glass windows prismed behind her, creating a colorful glow around her head. They began to sing one of Nathan's favorite hymns. Above all the other choir members, Paige's voice rang out clear and true. If he thought her singing had moved him before, it was nothing compared with her performance of this holy song. The same swell of emotion rose in his chest, threatening to suffocate him. He swallowed, forcing back the unwanted sensations.

By the time the pastor stood at the pulpit, Nathan had regained control of his emotions. He made himself concentrate on Reverend Redding's eloquent lesson about God's unconditional love and forgiveness, which touched Nathan in a profound way.

"Surrender your perceived sins to the Lord and let the Lord bear the burden."

The words echoed in Nathan's heart. If only it were that easy to give away all the pain, all the guilt, all the regret. Let God handle everything. Much easier said than done.

When the service was over, Nathan and Zach waited for Paige outside, watching the pastor greet his parishioners.

"Come on, Dad." Taking his hand, Zach dragged Nathan over to the minister.

"Hi, Pastor Dan," Zach greeted him. "This is my dad."

"Hello, Zach. Good to see you again." Pastor Dan smiled, ruffling Zach's hair.

Nathan held out his hand. "I'm Nathan Porter. Nice to meet you."

Dan was several inches shorter than Nathan, but his air of confidence gave him a larger-than-life presence.

"Dan Redding. You've got a great boy here."

"Thank you."

Dan's eyes turned serious. "Catherine Reynolds told me how you helped Paige out of a very bad situation. Let me tell you how grateful we all are."

A flash of heat rose up Nathan's neck. "I'm just thankful I was there."

Dan nodded. "So are we." He cocked his head, frowning. "You seem familiar. Have we met somewhere?"

A spurt of panic arrowed through Nathan. It was possible he'd met Dan at some clergy event. He prayed Dan didn't make the connection. Nathan was nowhere near ready to talk about why he'd left his ministry. "It's possible. I used to come to Wyndermere quite often."

He released a relieved breath when he spotted Paige coming to join them.

"Hi, Dan," she said. "I see you've all met."

"We have." Dan bent to kiss her cheek. "You look like you're feeling much better."

"I am. Thank you."

"And I must thank *you* for filling in today. You sounded wonderful as usual."

"I second the motion," Nathan added, welcoming the change in conversation.

Dan turned back to Nathan. "So, what are you doing with yourself while you're here?"

What did he do? His days meandered on without purpose. Nathan shrugged. "Basically relaxing. Reading, swimming, running—a little exercise every day. Oh, and eating too much. The dining room is excellent."

Dan laughed. "Sounds wonderful. I could use some R & R myself." He paused. "Do you golf at all?"

"I do. But I didn't bring my clubs."

"We have a pretty good course about five minutes away, and they rent clubs. Would you like to join me for a game tomorrow?"

Nathan waited a beat, not sure what to make of this unexpected invitation. The lure of some adult conversation and a good golf game finally won out. "I'd like that. Thanks."

"Great." Dan slapped him on the back. "I'll make reservations for seven a.m."

Paige's satisfied smile made Nathan wonder if he'd just been hoodwinked.

"I'm rustier than I thought." Dan laughed as he marked a score of five on the eighth hole the next day.

"Lucky for me or I'd be losing by a whole lot more." Nathan smiled, amazed to feel so relaxed.

It was the perfect weather for golf—sunny and warm, tempered with a light breeze. The course itself overflowed with pink flowering shrubs and tall shade trees that flanked the lush fairway. The intense color was enough to brighten anyone's mood.

If Nathan had been worried about being grilled by Dan, he needn't have. Dan was charming, funny and kept the conversation purposely light. At the halfway mark, Dan motioned Nathan over to a stone bench in the shade where they sat down. He opened a small cooler bag, pulled out two bottles of water and handed one to Nathan. They sat for a while in silence, enjoying their surroundings while another group of golfers played through.

At last Dan broke the stillness. "I was very sorry to hear about your recent loss. Paige told me a bit about what happened."

Despite his best effort, Nathan stiffened. "Thank you. It's been a difficult time."

Dan took a sip from the bottle. "I imagine Zach is taking it very hard."

It took great control for Nathan not to flinch at the stark sympathy on Dan's face, but he managed a nod.

"I understand Paige is working with him, helping him deal with his grief."

"That's right." Nathan replaced the cap on his bottle, hoping his terseness wouldn't offend the pastor.

"How's that going?"

Nathan ran a hand over his jaw. "Zach's improved quite a bit. But I'm not sure if it's real progress, or if he's just enjoying camp and forgetting about his mother for the moment."

Dan laid a hand on Nathan's shoulder. "In my experience with grieving kids, the healing process takes time. And it usually involves two steps forward, one step back." He stood up to throw his bottle in the trash, then picked up his golf bag. "Just give him time and love. That's the best you can do."

By the eighteenth hole, the midday sun blazed down

over the green. The final score was very close, but Nathan ended up ahead by two strokes.

"How about the winner buys you some lunch?" Nathan offered.

"You're on."

The restaurant inside the golf club had the perfect casual atmosphere. While they waited for their sandwiches, Dan chatted amiably about his life as a small-town pastor. Nathan listened, trying to quell the envy he felt for this man, who seemed so comfortable with himself and his career, and who had the support of a loving wife.

"Paige seems quite fond of you and Zach," Dan commented, before biting into his sandwich.

Nathan paused, unsure how to respond. He opted for neutrality. "Zach is very fond of her, as well." He took a bite of his burger, uneasy at the odd expression on the other man's face.

"And how about you, Nathan? How do you feel about Paige?"

Tension stiffened Nathan's spine. Why would he ask such a thing? "I admire her a great deal," he said carefully. "She's doing a wonderful thing for my son, and I'm grateful to her."

Dan took a sip of his drink. "Are you ever going to tell her you're a minister?"

Nathan's hand jerked and his iced tea sloshed over the rim of his glass.

"I finally figured out why you look so familiar," Dan went on. "I heard you speak at the Ecclesiastical Conference three years ago in New York. You were brilliant."

Nathan scowled as he mopped up the spill with a napkin. "I'm not a minister anymore."

Dan's eyes widened. "What do you mean?"

"I haven't been working since my wife—" He broke off and clamped his mouth shut.

"Since your wife died?"

He shook his head. "Before that. Since my wife left me."

Dan hid his surprise well. "I'm sorry. When did that happen?"

The inquiry was so gentle Nathan couldn't take offense. Instead he found himself wanting to confide in Dan.

"Cynthia left me six months before she died. Apparently she found someone who could dote on her day and night." He stopped. "I'm sorry. That was inappropriate."

Dan shook his head. "Don't apologize. Sounds like you have a lot of bottled-up anger you need to let out."

The statement hung in the air until Nathan dared look Dan in the eye. "I suppose I do. I'm just not sure that you're the right person to dump this on."

Dan didn't break eye contact. "It's your call, of course. But please consider that I might be the *perfect* person to talk to, since I have inside knowledge of what your life was like—the pressure of juggling the needs of your family and the obligation to your parishioners. Believe me, I know how hard that is, and my parish is nowhere near the size of yours."

Nathan could see the logic in his point, but still he hesitated.

"Tell you what," Dan continued. "You think about it and let me know what you decide."

Nathan smiled, relief loosening his tense muscles. "Thanks. I'll do that."

Dan continued to eat his lunch, but Nathan found his appetite gone. Looking over, he caught Dan eyeing him intently and knew the man had more on his mind.

"Paige and I have been friends for several years now," Dan said. "From what I know about her, honesty is something she values. If her opinion is important to you, I think you should tell her the truth about who you really are."

Chapter Ten

Paige lifted a box of ribbons onto the picnic table and squinted out over the expanse of sand at the group of kids playing on the beach. Each year, she looked forward to the annual church picnic, and this year was no exception. Lakeside Park, with its large beach area and acres of rolling grass, was the perfect setting.

If only she could get her mind off the stunning bit of news Zach had unwittingly revealed during their therapy chat the other day.

He'd started talking about church on Sunday and how fun it was to have his dad sit in the pew with him instead of being up front.

Paige had frowned at Zach. "Why did your dad sit up front?" Maybe Nathan was a church elder or someone who read the lessons.

Zach scrunched his nose. "The minister always sits up there."

Paige's mouth fell open. "Your dad's a minister?"

He looked up, his brown eyes unguarded. "He used to be. He hasn't been to church in a long time."

Paige's thoughts had gone into a tailspin, and she still couldn't quite wrap her brain around the idea. *Nathan was a minister?* She tried to remember what he'd said about his wife's problems with his demanding job. At the time, Paige had imagined him in a corporate setting and had sympathized with Cynthia's point of view. But now, knowing he'd been busy tending to the needs of his parishioners, the long hours away from his family took on a whole new perspective. From her dealings with Dan and Gwen Redding, Paige knew all too well the demands on a clergyman's time. It took a strong, understanding woman to share the man she loved with so many people. But Nathan's willingness to dedicate his time and attention to his congregation showed his strength and compassion, too.

"Earth to Paige."

Sandy's humor-filled voice snapped Paige back to the present. "Sorry about that. What's up?"

Sandy plopped down on the bench beside her with a dramatic sigh. "Jerry says the next race will start in about twenty minutes."

Paige looked over at Sandy and burst out laughing at her bedraggled appearance. Her friend's dark hair lay plastered to her head and her blouse clung to her like a second skin, revealing her bathing suit underneath. "I see you lost the water balloon toss."

"Nope. I got ambushed by the sore losers. Jerry led the attack." She rolled her eyes in mock disgust, then grinned.

"You loved every minute of it." Paige set the box on the grass. "I'd advise you to avoid the egg race, though. Could be messy."

"Don't give them any ideas." Sandy laughed as she twisted the water out of her shirt.

Paige was still chuckling when she noticed Nathan heading across the lawn toward them. Her heart did a loop-the-loop at the sight of him. She'd done a good job of avoiding him since the near-kiss incident. Now she pushed back her attraction and forced herself to remember her resolution not to get involved.

Nathan pulled off his sunglasses as he reached them. "Hello, ladies."

"Hi, Nathan." Sandy seemed amazingly unselfconscious about her soggy condition. "Enjoying yourself?"

He smiled. "Very much so. The kids are having a great time."

"Not only the kids." Paige looked pointedly at Sandy.

"What can I say? I'm a child at heart. And there's one big kid named Jerry that I need to take revenge on. See you two later." Sandy jumped up from the picnic bench and set off at a jog toward the beach.

Paige held back a sigh. Ever since Nathan had rescued her from Brandon, her friend had some misguided notion that she and Nathan were destined to be together. Paige, however, knew better.

"I was hoping to have a chance to talk to you today," Nathan said. "There's something I need to tell you."

The wind tousled his dark hair as he stood waiting for her response. He looked so serious, her pulse skipped. Surely he wouldn't want to discuss the almost-kiss. That was one topic best left alone.

"I've got two more races to supervise." She pushed the hair out of her eyes. "After that, I should be free for a bit."

He nodded. "Fine. I'll meet you then."

He turned away, his expression too solemn for Paige's liking.

"Nathan," she called, "does this have something to do with Zach?"

He looked over his shoulder, a frown wrinkling his brow. "Not really. I'll explain later."

And with that, he headed toward the crowd, leaving Paige to worry.

Nathan stood on the sidelines watching the egg race, his nerves as wobbly as the orbs on the spoons. Getting the courage to reveal his background to Paige was proving a lot harder than he'd imagined. Somehow this seemed more difficult than telling her about his wife's affair or their separation. Of course, he hadn't known Paige very well then, whereas now the stakes seemed so much higher because he valued her good opinion of him.

Reverend Nathan Porter. The title had defined the biggest part of his being. And explained why, without his career, he now questioned everything about himself. He'd failed not only at his marriage but at his life's vocation. Would Paige be disgusted by his cowardice at abandoning his calling? Would this admission cost him her respect? At the very least, she'd be angry with him for keeping this secret when she'd asked for his full disclosure on anything to do with him and Zach. He sighed. Either reaction would be gut-wrenching.

He took a moment to contemplate the enthusiastic group of people cheering on their children. The crowd served as another vivid reminder of what he'd missed since leaving his position at the church—the camaraderie of parishioners, the sense of community and family spirit. But what he missed even more was his own spirituality. Going back to church, even for one day, had been like giving a starving man a piece of bread. One small taste made him yearn for more.

"Your son won the egg race."

Nathan blinked at Mrs. Appleby, a plump, grandmotherly type, standing beside him.

"You'd better go congratulate him."

He smiled. "Thank you, Mrs. Appleby."

But Zach beat him to it, running across the field toward him, a blue ribbon clutched in his hand. With an excited cry, he flung himself into Nathan's arms. "Look, Dad. I won first place!"

"Congratulations." Nathan had mere seconds to relish the wiry arms around his neck before Zach pulled away to admire his prize.

"She's a beauty." Nathan ruffled his son's hair.

"I'm going to pin it on the wall beside my bunk when we get back. I've never won anything before." His eyes shone with happiness.

A rush of emotion surged in Nathan's chest as he recalled the angry boy he'd brought with him only a few weeks ago. "I'm proud of you, Zach."

"Thanks, Dad." Zach gave him another strangling hug, then scampered down. "Gotta go. See you later."

"Be careful."

Nathan watched his son race over to the group of kids gathered on the beach and took a minute to collect himself. The fact that Zach had wanted to share his excitement with him touched Nathan deeply.

"You and Zach seem to be getting along better."

Paige's quiet voice startled him. He hadn't heard her come up from behind. Struggling to compose his features, he turned. "Seems that way. I hope it lasts."

"I'm sure it will." She held out a paper cup. "I brought you some lemonade."

"Thanks." He took the cup and gulped down a large appreciative mouthful.

"I have to get some supplies from Dan's van. Do you want to walk with me so we can talk?"

"Sure." He drained his cup and threw it in the trash. "Lead the way."

They headed across a field in the direction of the parking lot, walking in silence at first. Nathan stared at the grass as he walked, unsure how to begin.

"How was your golf game with Dan?"

He glanced up, grateful for an opening. "It was fun. I think he let me win though."

She laughed. "I doubt it. Dan may be sweet, but he has a definite competitive edge."

"Well, I enjoyed it."

The wind blew a few strands of hair across Paige's face. "Did you find Dan easy to talk to?"

If Nathan weren't so apprehensive, he would've laughed at her obvious attempt to learn what had transpired between them. Instead he smothered a smile and nodded. "Dan is very skilled at getting people to open up about themselves."

He stopped at a picnic table and motioned for her to sit down.

She gave him a puzzled look as she took a seat. "What's the matter, Nathan? You don't seem yourself today."

With a sigh, he sat down beside her, clasping his hands between his knees. "I have a confession to make, and I hope when you hear me out, you'll forgive me for not telling you sooner."

The faint flutter of nerves quivered in Paige's stomach. She couldn't imagine what Nathan was about to say, but from the look on his face, she didn't imagine it could be anything good. His dark eyebrows drew together in a frown as he stared out over the rolling greenery.

"Go ahead," she said. "I'm listening."

He turned to face her, eyes troubled. It surprised her how much she wanted to smooth the hair from his forehead and erase the ridges of worry furrowed there.

"I know you've been wondering what I do for a living," he said, "and why I haven't wanted to talk about it."

She stiffened on the hard wooden planks. The fact that she already knew filled her with guilt. "Nathan, you don't have to—"

"Yes, I do." Agitation laced his words. "It's a huge part of what's been holding me back from healing and from moving on with my life. Unless I can talk about it, I'll never get past this."

On a deep exhale, he pushed off the table and strode over to a nearby tree. The depth of his pain showed in his bowed head and hunched shoulders. Paige watched him with a heavy heart, wishing she could offer him comfort. What had brought about this sudden need to confess?

At last he turned to face her, his hands clenched into fists at his side. "I used to be a minister."

The words hung in the air and she struggled for the appropriate reaction. "Used to be? As in, you're not anymore?"

He shook his head, and the misery on his face pinched her heart.

"I've been on an extended leave of absence. I don't know when, or if, I'll ever go back."

Paige got down from the table and went to stand in front of him. "Now I have a confession to make. I already knew you're a minister. Zach mentioned it after church last Sunday."

Nathan frowned. "Why didn't you say anything?"

She shrugged. "It wasn't my place. I figured if you wanted me to know, you'd tell me yourself."

He stared at her for a few seconds and Paige forced herself to breathe normally. She hoped he didn't think she'd used Zach to pry into his business.

"Why did you have to leave your position?" she finally asked.

His gaze dropped to the ground, and they started walking again. "After Cynthia left, I felt like a fraud."

"How so?" They reached Dan's minivan and Paige opened the back hatch.

Nathan lifted a cardboard box of supplies out of the trunk and set it on the ground. "I was so consumed with rage, I couldn't write my weekly sermons. How could I talk about forgiveness and love when I was filled with bitterness and, at times, even hatred?" He slammed the hatch door closed.

She leaned back against the van. "Those feelings were only normal after what you'd been through."

He threw out his hands, then let them drop. "But I was a man of God. If I couldn't overcome a personal crisis by relying on my faith, how could I expect anyone else to?" Anguish ravaged his face.

Paige placed her hand on his arm. "I'm so sorry, Nathan. What a nightmare that must have been."

Nathan shook his head, frowning.

"What is it?" Had she said the wrong thing?

"I thought you'd be furious with me for keeping this from you. Instead you're trying to make me feel better."

Suddenly self-conscious, she busied herself gathering up the bags of hot dog buns. "Somebody has to. You're far too hard on yourself."

"No, I mean it. You wanted me to be honest with you to help Zach, but I withheld a big piece of the picture."

A ridiculous prickle of happiness touched her that he was so worried she'd be upset with him. "I'm not mad, Nathan. I'm just glad you felt you could confide in me."

"Thank you for understanding." The gruffness of his voice resonated inside her.

"You're welcome."

Nathan picked up the carton, and Paige fell into step beside him as they started back. She thought about the irony of the situation when she'd wondered if he was a churchgoer or not, and couldn't help chuckling.

"What's so funny?"

"I can't believe I was trying to get you to go to church and all along you were a minister."

Nathan chuckled himself. "That crossed my mind, too." He sobered. "I should have told you right then, but I just couldn't do it."

"What made you tell me now?"

He shifted the weight of the box and glanced over at her. "Dan recognized me. He'd heard me speak at a conference a couple of years ago. It was his suggestion that I should tell you, that you would probably understand."

"I told you Dan was a good person to talk to. He's very wise for his age and a good listener."

"They used to say that about me." Nathan's smile was tinged with sadness.

"And they will again. Once you get over this crisis, you'll be a better resource than ever for your parishioners because you've dealt with the same issues."

A small cloud of dirt drifted up from the path as they walked. "I still don't know if I can go back."

At last she understood the full extent of his pain, his self-doubt, his loss of confidence. "Be patient with yourself, Nathan. Wounds that deep take time to heal."

He shook his head. "My leave is almost up and my superiors need an answer very soon."

He stopped walking as they reached the picnic area, seeming reluctant to rejoin the crowd.

"Would you consider talking to Dan again...professionally?" Paige asked softly.

The sound of children's laughter floated over to them as she waited for his reply.

He set the box down on a nearby bench. "Dan offered to counsel me. I told him I'd think about it."

She smiled, knowing in her heart that, given the opportunity, God would speak to Nathan through Dan. "I don't think it could hurt. Dan's the least judgmental person I know, and he always seems to say just the right thing to put things in perspective."

Nathan nodded. "Good to know."

She took a step back and purposely lightened the mood. "Now that we've got all that settled, you need to go and have some fun with your son. If not, I'm putting you to work at the barbecue."

He grinned and gave a mock salute. "Yes, ma'am."

* * *

Nathan felt a huge weight had lifted from his soul. Once again, Paige had amazed him with her innate compassion. She had a way of making him feel at ease, of feeling that any actions he took were all perfectly natural. Her calm acceptance without censure was a gift.

After dropping the supplies at the picnic area, Nathan made his way to the ball diamond to find Zach. Perhaps he'd join the game in progress. His heart lightened at the prospect. It had been years since he'd played baseball. Years since he'd done anything simply for fun.

As Nathan approached the field, he noticed an older couple on the sidelines near the bleachers, cheering on the players. The sight of the woman's flamboyant blouse, over-size sunglasses and high heels stopped Nathan cold.

It couldn't be.

The woman removed her glasses, and Nathan's stomach clenched in dread. What were the MacNeals doing here? Whatever reason brought Cynthia's parents here, it couldn't be good.

He squared his shoulders in preparation for battle, fixed a neutral expression on his face and moved forward. "Charlotte. Ted. This is a surprise." He bent to kiss Charlotte's cheek and shook Ted's outstretched hand.

Ted wore a friendly smile. However, Charlotte's mouth remained turned down at the corners.

"We read on the website that today was Family Fun Day for the camp, in association with the church," she said, "so we decided to come for a visit."

A six-hour drive just for a picnic? No, there had to be more to this visit than that. "Does Zach know you're here?"

"Oh, yes. He was thrilled to see us. Made sure we'd watch him at bat."

Nathan stood with them, his jaw tight, all thoughts of joining the game blown away. He wasn't sure what his in-laws were up to, but he wouldn't leave them alone long enough to create any havoc.

From second base, Zach jumped and waved. "Hi, Dad. Look, I made a hit."

"Good job," he called back.

Beside him, Charlotte waved madly at his son.

"I'm glad you're here," Nathan said a few minutes later, when the teams switched positions and Zach headed to the outfield with Peter. "You can see for yourself how much better Zach is doing."

Charlotte turned her head toward him. "That's exactly why we're here. You didn't think we'd let the whole summer go by without checking on our grandson, did you? Hauling him off to some unruly place in the country." She sniffed as though the air smelled of manure or some such unpleasantness, then pushed her glasses on top of her head to pierce him with a haughty stare. "Other than playing games in the wilderness, what steps have you taken to ensure Zachary's emotional well-being?"

Nathan's tongue pasted to the roof of his mouth. All the words of calm assurance he wanted to say drifted from his mind. "Well, as a matter of fact, Zach has been talking to a therapist."

"A therapist? Up here?" She waved her hand as though Sigmund Freud himself would step out from between the trees.

Nathan took a deep breath, determined not to let the woman get the best of his temper as she had so often in the past. "That's right. And I'm happy to tell you that Zach has made a great deal of improvement in the short time he's been here."

"You expect me to take your word for that?"

Ted stepped forward to place an arm around his wife. "Now, Charlotte, you promised no fighting. We're here to spend some time with Zach."

"And we will. But not before I get some proof of Nathan's claim."

Waves of nausea forced their way up Nathan's throat. He half expected a lawyer to appear with a court order.

"I'd be more than happy to verify his statement." Paige seemed to come out of nowhere.

Nathan almost sagged with relief. He'd been so intent on the battle of wills, he hadn't even noticed her arrive.

Charlotte fisted a hand on her hip. "And who are you, may I ask?"

"This is Paige McFarlane, the camp director. Paige, this is Charlotte and Ted MacNeal, Zach's grandparents."

Paige smiled widely as she shook each of their hands. "So nice to meet you. I'm sure Zach is excited you're here."

Charlotte frowned, her thin eyebrows cinching. "I don't understand. You are the camp counselor. Not a therapist. How can you verify anything other than Zach's ball-playing prowess?"

Paige's expression remained pleasant. "I am also acting as a grief therapist for Zach."

"What type of qualifications could a camp counselor have?"

Nathan watched Paige's shoulders stiffen. "I'm finishing a master's degree in child psychology. I've studied grief therapy as well as childhood mental health issues."

Charlotte's mouth dropped open. "Mental health?"

"Depression and anger are common components of the grieving process." Paige's voice softened. "You yourselves, I'm sure, have experienced this since the loss of your daughter. The only difference is that children aren't as well equipped to handle such intense emotions. We give them tools to cope with their overwhelming feelings."

To Nathan's surprise, Charlotte seemed at a loss for words.

"Let me assure you that Zach is making good progress,

and I will continue working with him as long as he's here."
Paige motioned to Nathan. "Nathan has been very supportive through the whole process."

Charlotte raised her chin. "Supportive? I highly doubt
that. Did he tell you how he all but abandoned his son when
he and my daughter separated? That he hasn't been working for almost a year? And that while under his care, Zach
got suspended twice for attacking a classmate? What kind
of father is that?"

Bile rose in the back of Nathan's throat, making speech
impossible. He could not deny any one of his former
mother-in-law's claims.

Paige took a step closer to Charlotte. "Any man who has
undergone the type of trauma that Nathan has endured over
the last year is entitled to our compassion and support, not
criticism or attempts to undermine his place in his son's
life. He is working hard to get over this tragedy while seeking help for his son. That's more than a lot of people would
do in similar circumstances. I, for one, admire Nathan for
taking the time to process his grief before attempting to
move on with his life."

Nathan was stunned to see tight lines of anger on Paige's
face. Anger on his behalf. Never had anyone defended him
so fiercely.

Charlotte snapped her mouth shut. A roar from the spec-
tators behind them turned their attention to the game. One
of the boys had hit a long ball and was rounding the bases.
In the outfield, Zach and Peter chased the ball.

Paige took a breath and moved back. "I suggest that you
put your differences aside for the time being, and for Zach's
sake, enjoy the rest of the day with him."

Ted nodded vigorously. "I agree one hundred percent,
young lady."

Paige's gaze shifted from Ted back to Charlotte. "If you
need a professional report on Zach's progress, I'd be more

than happy to provide one at the end of camp. Just leave me the address and I'll make sure you get a copy."

She looked at Nathan for the first time. He wasn't sure what emotions he saw swirling in the depths of her eyes. "If you need me for anything, I'll be helping with the food."

"Thank you." He hoped those two simple words could somehow convey the depth of his gratitude.

Paige had managed to defuse a potentially volatile situation and get Charlotte to back down. No small feat. For the first time in months, the perceived threat of the MacNeals taking Zach away from him lessened. The tight muscles in his chest relaxed, allowing him to breathe a little easier.

And Nathan owed it all to Paige.

Chapter Eleven

Early Monday morning, Paige awakened to the sound of rain pelting the cabin roof above her. With a groan, she pushed out of bed and grabbed her clipboard to begin planning a day of indoor activities for the kids. The growing intensity of the wind rattled the walls while she worked, and a knot of worry formed in her stomach. This storm seemed worse than any she remembered at Wyndermere. Would these old cabins hold out against Mother Nature's wrath?

When her cell phone chirped on her nightstand a few minutes past seven, Paige knew it would be George.

"Hey, boss. What's up?"

"Get all the kids over to the inn as soon as possible. Ask a parent to stay with them in the auditorium. Emergency staff meeting in fifteen minutes."

His terse voice sent shivers of apprehension through her. "Got it."

Sandy emerged from the bathroom, a worried frown on her face. "Who was that?"

"George. Emergency staff meeting. Let's get the kids up."

Paige and Sandy helped the girls dress and pack a few personal items in their backpacks, while fighting to keep the concern from showing on their faces.

"Everybody into your rain gear." Paige pulled on her own jacket, sending Sandy a worried glance. She gathered her pack and a flashlight and pulled up the hood of her raincoat. "I'm going to check on Jerry and the boys, then I'll join you at the inn."

Sandy nodded.

"Okay. Everyone hold hands. Let's go."

The wind whipped the door out of Paige's hand as soon as she turned the handle, slamming it back against the cabin wall. It took all her strength to wrestle it closed again once everyone had exited.

Rain slashed at her face and the wind pummeled her until she reached the other cabin. Not bothering to knock, she flung the door open and stepped inside, bringing a torrent of water with her. The boys stood in a row along the wall, looking very serious.

Jerry glanced up from zipping his orange rain slicker, relief spilling over his features. "I'm glad you're here. Can you take the boys to the inn? George wants me down at the docks to secure the boats."

"Sure." She wiped the moisture from her eyes. "Be careful out there. That wind is ferocious."

"I will."

Paige frowned, nerves dancing in her stomach. This storm had a dangerous feel to it. "It's bad, isn't it?" She kept her voice low so as not to upset the boys.

Somber eyes masked Jerry's usual lighthearted personality. "Tornado watch. George will fill you in."

A few minutes later, Paige and the very soggy boys entered the auditorium. Right away, she spied Nathan standing with Sandy by the stage. When Zach raced over to hug his father, Nathan didn't hesitate to clasp him up, wet coat and all, and whisper what were likely reassurances in his ear.

Nathan looked over and caught her eye. He set Zach down and proceeded across the room toward her.

"How bad is it?" he asked.

"Bad enough. I'll know more once George briefs us."

He handed her a handkerchief from his pocket to wipe her face. That was the type of man he was—the type who carried handkerchiefs.

"Thanks. What are you doing down here?"

"Sandy asked me to help out with the kids while you go to your meeting. A couple of other parents should be down soon."

Paige darted a glance around the room. "Where are the MacNeals? Have they left to go home?"

"They left last night." He stepped closer. "I never got the chance to thank you properly for what you said to them."

Paige squirmed under his admiring gaze. "All I did was tell the truth." She handed him back the handkerchief, which he pocketed.

"All the same, it helped defuse the situation. And it meant a lot to me that you defended Zach and me like that."

"You're welcome." His words of approval warmed the deep places in her heart. Maybe she was doing something right after all.

Sandy joined them. "We'd better get to the meeting or George will have our heads." She scanned the room, frowning. "Where's Jerry?"

"Down at the docks securing the boats."

Sandy's eyes widened in alarm. "It's way too dangerous out there with that wind."

Paige quirked a brow. Since when was Sandy so concerned about Jerry's well-being? "He'll be fine. He has other guys helping him. Come on. Let's find out what we're dealing with."

They walked in to see George standing in a military-like posture at the front of the conference room. Once everyone had arrived, he relayed the news with terse precision. The weather station warned of gale-force winds with the possibility of tornadoes in the area. Looking around the room, Paige found every face as white and grim as her own must be. She thanked God for a leader like George, who kept a level head in times of crisis.

"Staff will evacuate all guests to the basement and divide them between the employee cafeteria and the auditorium. Outdoor crews will secure the patio furniture and any other items that might prove hazardous. The maintenance crew and any other volunteers will board up windows as long as it remains safe to do so." George scanned the group. "We need flashlights, batteries, portable radios and anything else that would be helpful if the power goes out. I will personally see that the emergency generator is online. We'll keep in touch by cell phones and walkie-talkies."

After making sure everyone was certain of the assigned duties, George dismissed the staff. A silent group filed out. Paige waited to give George's arm an encouraging squeeze.

"This might be a good time to get your prayers going," he commented grimly, then pushed out the door.

Thankfully, the kids viewed the storm as a grand adventure, and after a few games in the auditorium, Paige settled them on the floor with a video. Once the movie started, she headed to the cafeteria to grab a coffee.

Sandy followed her in. "Is your cell phone working? My battery died."

"I'm not sure. Why?"

"Jerry's still not back. Can you try him for me?"

Paige set her mug on the counter and pulled out her phone. But Jerry didn't answer. She left a message asking him to call her.

"He's probably too busy to pick up." Paige looked up, astounded to see tears in her friend's eyes. She fisted a hand on her hip as suspicion whispered through her. "Is there something I should know about you and Jerry? Because if I recall, you could barely tolerate him last summer."

Sandy blushed and looked away, hugging her arms to her body. "I guess the guy kinda grew on me."

"Grew on you? As in you can stand to be in the same room with him, or as in you're madly in love with him?"

Sandy groaned. "I don't know."

A slow grin twitched Paige's lips. "I don't believe it. My two best friends are in love."

"Shh. Shh." Sandy's fingers dug into Paige's arm. "I don't know how Jerry feels. You have to swear not to say anything."

"Okay, I promise." Paige leaned over to hug her friend. "Don't worry, he'll be fine."

"I hope you're right," Sandy said, "because if he's not back soon, I'm going out after him."

Sandy's admission did a lot to brighten Paige's day, giving her something positive to focus on. The movie was almost over when she looked up to see Nathan standing in the doorway. He squinted as if adjusting to the dim lighting inside. Even in a raincoat and rubber boots, he exuded masculinity.

"Everything okay here?" he asked, his gaze on Zach.

"Fine. What have you been doing?"

"Helping out where I could. We got most of the lakeside windows boarded up. They've gone to do the same at George's house. I wanted to check on Zach before I joined them."

"He's fine, but he'll be glad to see you." Paige pushed some stray hairs behind her ear, suddenly self-conscious in her old jeans and sweatshirt. "Did you happen to see Jerry out there?"

"He was helping with the windows last I saw him. Why?"

She shrugged. "Sandy and I were worried. Have you had anything to eat?"

He gave a tired smile. "A soggy sandwich and some coffee."

"I could get you something from the kitchen."

"Thanks, but I should go. Tell Zach I'll be back later." Nathan hesitated, his gaze locked with hers, as though he wanted to say more.

Be careful. The words trembled on Paige's tongue, but she only nodded.

The door flew open and George stalked in, his weathered face contorted in a scowl.

"Nathan," he called, motioning him over. "I need your help."

Sensing a new problem, Paige followed Nathan.

George shook the water from his jacket. "I had a call from Dan Redding. There's trouble down at the church. He needs any help he can get."

"What kind of trouble?" Paige's thoughts flew to Dan's wife, Gwen, and their two young boys.

"An old elm tree crashed through one of the church's windows. Took part of the wall with it." His grim eyes matched the lines bracketing his mouth.

Paige gasped. "Was anyone hurt?"

"No, but rain's getting inside, causing all kinds of damage. They need to get the tree out and patch the hole before the whole place floods."

"Count me in." Nathan zipped up his coat.

"Me, too."

"No!" Both men whirled on her.

She fisted her hands on her hips. "Why not?"

George scowled. "It's not safe out there. Besides, you're needed here with the kids." Turning, he looped an arm around Nathan's shoulders. "We'll need ropes, work gloves and saws."

His voice trailed away as they disappeared through the door, leaving Paige stewing in the hall. She loved that church, and Dan and Gwen were her friends. She would not sit idly by when they needed her. Thoughts racing, she turned to find Sandy behind her.

"What's going on?"

"Jerry's okay," Paige said quickly to allay her fear. "Nathan saw him boarding up windows. But Dan needs help at the church. Would you mind if I went?"

"No, you go on. I've got lots of parents to help with the kids. But be careful, please."

She hugged Sandy hard. "I will. Thanks."

Grabbing her rain gear, Paige raced down the hall.

At the side entrance of the inn, Paige stopped to pull on her boots and tie her hood under her chin, before pushing out into the storm. The wind was even stronger than earlier—the rain just as fierce. Trees swayed and bent almost in two. Loose debris, litter, garbage cans—anything not tied down—blew by.

Paige wished her secondhand Volkswagen hadn't died on her two months ago. Squinting through the downpour, she saw a group of men in raincoats getting into two pickups, and recognized one of the maintenance guys. She ran over in his direction, grateful Nathan and George had already left.

"Tim," she bellowed over the din of the storm. "Are you heading to the church?"

"Yup."

"Can I hitch a ride with you?"

He hesitated for a second, then shrugged. "Hop in."

She jumped up and squeezed into the back of the cab. Two more men piled in and Tim jerked the truck into motion.

After a rough ride into town, Paige breathed a relieved sigh when he pulled up in front of the church. Relief turned to dismay, however, at the sight of a large tree trunk protruding from the wall of the church. A group of men wielding chain saws worked at a furious pace. Paige recognized George, Nathan and Dan among them. Hoping to avoid her boss's wrath for the moment, she hunched against the storm's onslaught, and made her way to the rectory.

Gwen Redding answered on the second knock, pushing her short blond hair off her forehead.

"Paige," she exclaimed. "Come in, quick."

She pulled her in and wrestled the door shut. Paige shrugged out of her drenched raincoat and gave Gwen a hug. "How are you holding up?"

"I'm a little frazzled, but it's not been too bad. The boys are getting cabin fever though."

"Tell me about it. I've got a whole pack of them back at Wyndermere."

Gwen laughed and gestured her to follow. "Come back to the kitchen. I'm on coffee detail."

Paige surveyed two large coffee urns on the counter. "How can I help?"

"You can stir the hot chocolate for me. That big pot on the stove."

Paige picked up the wooden spoon and began to stir the brown liquid while Gwen poured coffee into large silver thermoses.

"I'm so sorry about the church. Will insurance cover the damage?"

"It should. We want to save the pews if we can. There's a whole crew working on the inside, bailing water and clearing debris."

"I'm going over in a few minutes, but I wanted to see you guys first."

The sound of running feet caused Paige to look over her shoulder. She grinned as two blond boys scampered into the kitchen.

"Hi, Paige." Johnny grinned. At six years old, he was a natural-born leader.

"Hi, boys." Paige ruffled their hair. It had been too long since she'd spent time with Gwen and the kids. She missed the mischievous imps.

Four-year-old Alex stared up at her with serious brown eyes. "We're watching for a 'nado."

Johnny snorted. "Not a ''nado,' dummy. A tornado."

"That's what I said." Alex frowned.

"I don't think we're going to have a tornado," Paige said. "Just a lot of wind."

"But we *want* to see one!" Johnny bounced from one foot to the other. "Did you know they can pick up a truck and make it fly in the air?" His eyes went wide with excitement.

"Yes, we know," Gwen assured him, while Paige stifled another grin. "You go back to your lookout. If you see one coming, make sure you let us know."

"We will, Mama." He looked over at Paige. "We've got flashlights and everything in the basement."

She laughed. "Good man. You're ready for anything."

The excited boys raced off to their post.

Gwen wiped the perspiration from her forehead. "Could you bring these thermoses out to the men for me when you go?"

"Of course. Are you sure you don't need me to stay here?" Paige was torn by concern for her friend—who was obviously feeling the strain of the day—and her desire to help at the church.

"I'm fine. Give Dan a kiss for me if you see him, okay?"

Paige couldn't help but laugh as she pulled on her rain-coat. "Wouldn't that give the parishioners fuel for gossip?"

Carrying four large thermoses, Paige battled her way over to the church, careful to avoid the men sawing the tree. Truth be told, she didn't know which was more daunting, the possibility of a tornado, or facing the wrath of George and Nathan.

* * *

Nathan's arm muscles burned from exertion as he paused to wipe the rivulets of water from his eyes. He looked across the church lawn to the wood chipper, and a figure carrying some metal thermoses caught his attention. He squinted to peer through the stinging downpour.

Paige? What on earth was she doing here after George had expressly told her to stay at Wyndermere?

He threw down his saw and marched in her direction. He knew the moment she realized it was him by the way her eyes widened and she pivoted toward the church. Her foot had barely touched the first step when Nathan grabbed her by the arm and whirled her around.

"What are you doing here?" Rivers of water streamed down his face, almost blinding him. The wind howled around them, whipping his coat tight against him.

"I came to help," she yelled.

"It's too dangerous. Go back to Wyndermere."

She scowled and yanked her arm. The rain-slicked material slid from his grasp.

"Dan and Gwen are my friends, and I'm going to help them." She stormed up the stairs and flung open the door to the church.

A flash of exasperation bubbled through Nathan's chest. His anger propelled him up the stairs after her, but when he reached the door, reality hit him. He had no right to dictate her actions—not even under the guise of friendship.

Besides, he couldn't cause a scene in front of all the people working inside. He wouldn't embarrass Paige, or himself, like that.

Instead he stalked down the stairs and back to his spot at the tree. He put the energy of his frustration into the saw, amazed that steam wasn't evident from the friction he applied. What was she thinking following them out here? Putting herself in harm's way?

"Paige is a stubborn one," George yelled over the noise of the chain saws. The grim line of his mouth matched Nathan's mood. "No point in worrying about it now."

Nathan didn't bother to reply but continued the frantic rhythm of his sawing.

Dan passed behind them with a load of wood. "Give her a break, guys. Paige isn't the type to sit on the sidelines. She needs to be involved."

Nathan gave him a piercing glare. "Would you want Gwen out here?"

Dan frowned. "No."

"Exactly."

A big chunk of wood fell at Nathan's feet, which he kicked out of the way. When he looked up, Paige came into view, lugging an armful of branches to the wood chipper. He quelled the instinct to rush over and relieve her of her burden. She'd made it perfectly clear that his interference would not be tolerated.

Instead he turned back, picked up his saw and attacked the wood with a vengeance.

And tried to ignore the speculative look on Dan Redding's face.

"Take a break, honey. You've been going nonstop."

A plump middle-aged woman led Paige to a pew covered by a tarp to protect the wood. Grateful for the chance to sit down, she sank onto the hard surface. Her feet and back ached from lugging branches, and her arms quivered like limp noodles. She blew out a long breath, frowning as she recalled Nathan's furious face when he demanded that she return to Wyndermere. Why did he care that she was here? Was he worried about a lack of supervision for Zach? She didn't dare consider it could be anything else.

For a brief moment, Paige closed her eyes and allowed herself to float, listening to the many sounds around her.

It was then she detected the subtle change in the wind, the slight increase in intensity. She doubted anyone else had noticed—they were all too intent on their tasks. She rose and took deliberate steps out the door. As she suspected, the sky had taken on an eerie quality. An odd greenish light glowed from within the rolling clouds. She remembered seeing a sky like this once before when she was a child—the day a tornado touched down.

Her heart roared as fast as the wind. There wasn't much time. Her breath came in gasps as she tore up the stairs, back into the church.

"Tornado's coming. Everyone into the basement," she yelled.

All activity stopped and a moment of stunned silence followed before the men and women took action. Immediately, Paige raced back outside, almost tripping over her own feet. The rain had eased off, but far more disturbing was the wind that swirled about her in a circular pattern. Leaves, paper and dirt danced in the air above her head. Blocking her face with her arms, she raced over to George and Nathan.

"Get everyone inside." She grabbed George's arm and pointed at the sky.

"I'll get the others," he shouted above the gale.

"Where's Dan?"

"Inside the church, I think."

Paige's thoughts flew to Gwen and the boys. Had anyone warned them? Paige pivoted, only to find Nathan blocking her path.

"Where are you going?" The wind had torn off his hood, leaving his hair to blow freely, his face as thunderous as the sky.

"To warn Gwen."

"I'll go with you."

She didn't waste time arguing. The gales grew stronger by the minute. Nathan clamped his arm around her waist, and together they ran toward the house. He managed to wrench the front door open and bang it shut after they entered.

"Gwen," Paige called. Not bothering to remove her boots, she ran into the kitchen.

Gwen looked up from the stove, startled.

"Tornado's coming," Paige gasped out.

Gwen's eyes grew wide with alarm. "Where's Dan?"

Paige wasn't about to tell Gwen she didn't know for sure. "In the church. Don't worry, he'll be fine."

Without a word, Gwen turned off the burner under a big pot, put the lid on and followed Paige into the living room, where the two kids sat playing video games.

"Come on, boys. Let's go down to the basement."

Gwen scooped Alex into her arms, while Paige waited for Johnny. The windows rattled as wildly as Paige's nerves.

"Is it a tornado?" Excitement glowed in Johnny's eyes.

"I don't know, honey." Paige tried to answer in a calm voice, despite her racing heart. "We need to be safe just in case."

The boy tucked his hand in hers, and they headed to the stairs.

"Do you have a flashlight, a radio, batteries?" Nathan asked over his shoulder.

Gwen nodded. "Everything's in the basement. First door on the right."

The walls of the house literally shook as the group descended the stairs to the gloom below. A single bulb illuminated the cold gray walls and cement floor. The musty air seemed to shroud them as they entered. Johnny broke free from Paige's grasp and ran to his mother.

Paige moved to the middle of the room. Thankfully, there were no windows in the immediate area. They should be safe here. Gwen grabbed a stack of blankets from the

corner and spread them into two thick sitting areas on the
hard floor. With Alex on her lap and Johnny squeezed tight
to her side, Gwen cuddled her family, murmuring words
of comfort.

Nathan found the flashlights on a metal table and
checked them for battery strength. He opened his raincoat
and pulled out his cell phone. Scowling, he stuffed it back
in his pocket. "No signal down here."

Paige raised a weary hand to push back her soaked hood.
She wanted to assure Nathan that Zach would be safe at
Wyndermere, but spots danced before her eyes. "I think
I need to sit down," she whispered a second before her
knees gave way.

Nathan lunged, his strong arms grabbing her before she
hit the ground. Gently, he lowered her to a pile of blankets
on the floor.

"Gwen, do you have any water?" His eyes never left
Paige's face as he unzipped her jacket.

"In the cooler by the wall."

He went to get a bottle, cracked the lid and handed it to
her, shadows dancing over his pinched features.

She took several long gulps before handing it back.
"Thank you."

Nathan frowned and captured her hand. "You're bleeding."

She stared at the bloody gashes covering the backs of
both hands as if they belonged to someone else.

"There's a first-aid kit on the table," Gwen offered.

Nathan retrieved the box, removed an antiseptic wipe
and began to clean her wounds. The warmth of his hands
seeped into her chilled ones. He checked the palms, his fingers whispering over hers, then lightly rubbed salve into
the cuts and bandaged the bigger lesions. Paige trembled at
the tenderness in his touch. When he finished, she raised
her eyes to meet his intense stare, and her breath tangled

in her lungs from the sheer force of emotion vibrating between them.

Suddenly, a great roar, like a Learjet hovering over the roof, shattered the space. The entire house shook and groaned. The lightbulb flickered once, and then gave a loud pop, plunging them into total darkness.

Alex and Johnny shrieked, their terror palpable. Paige's nerves stretched to near breaking, and she clutched the soft cotton of Nathan's shirt. He gathered her into his arms and sat with her on the blankets. In the anonymity of darkness, she took comfort from his solid presence, pressing her face against the warmth of his chest, where his steady heartbeat soothed her.

Dear God, please keep us all safe. Let this tornado pass us by without harming anyone.

The deafening roar seemed to rage on indefinitely until it appeared the house would surely cave in under the pressure. Then, as abruptly as the noise had started, everything went still.

Paige lifted her head, listening for the next onslaught. After several minutes of eerie silence, she dared to hope the worst was over. The boys switched on the flashlights, and two beams of light cut a path through the darkness, focusing in on Paige and Nathan. She squinted against the glare, suddenly conscious of her proximity to Nathan. She tried to move away, but he held her fast.

"Do you think it's safe to go up?" Gwen asked in a hushed tone.

"Not yet," Nathan said. "Let's give it a bit longer to be sure."

Paige knew Gwen was terrified for her husband and prayed Dan and the others were uninjured. As if sensing Paige's fear, Nathan kept his arm around her, holding her snug against him. A few minutes later, pounding footsteps above them interrupted the silence. Gwen shot to her feet, a flashlight aimed at the foot of the stairs.

"Gwen? Johnny? Alex?" Dan's frantic voice preceded him into the room.

A strangled cry escaped Gwen. The flashlight clattered to the ground as she threw herself into her husband's arms. The sound of her sobs echoed in the small space. Both boys ran to join their parents, hugging the legs of the entwined pair.

"Thank God," Paige whispered, unaware of the tears that streamed down her face until they dripped off her chin.

Dan gave his wife a passionate kiss, one almost too intimate to witness, then turned to hug his children close. "Everyone all right?"

"Fine." Nathan helped Paige to her feet. "How about everyone else?"

"No injuries as far as I know."

"Did you see the 'nado, Daddy?" Alex asked.

"No, son. I didn't. We were very lucky it didn't touch down here. Came pretty close though."

"How's George?" Paige wiped the moisture from her cheeks.

"George and the others are fine. They're in the church basement."

"Any damage?" Nathan asked.

"Some. I'll have to do a thorough check later. But first, let's get out of here."

After holding her close during the storm, Nathan hated to let Paige go, especially when she seemed so shaky. But his first priority had to be Zach's safety. Once Paige was in Gwen's capable hands, he set out to find George. The battery for Nathan's phone had died while they were inside, and he prayed George had heard something from Wyndermere.

George, along with some of the other men, had just

emerged from the church as they arrived. "Nathan, Dan. Is everyone all right?"

"They're fine," Dan told him.

"Have you contacted Wyndermere yet?" Nathan asked.

George walked toward them. "No signal in the basement. I'm going to try again now."

He whipped out his cell phone and punched in the numbers. A few seconds later, relief spread over his craggy features. "Catherine, honey. You're all right?" He waited. "That's good news. Yes, we're all fine here."

They spoke for a few minutes more, with George doing most of the listening. Nathan could barely contain his impatience until the end of the call.

"Everyone is safe and sound," George told them at last. "The tornado, or whatever it was, missed them."

Nathan released the breath he'd been holding.

"Catherine has gone to tell Zach that you and Paige are okay."

"Thank you."

George clapped him on the back. "Let's finish this job so we can go home."

It took the crew another hour and a half to finally get the tree out of the church. By the time the last of the wood had been cleared, Nathan ached all over. Inside, however, he felt better than he had for a long time—needed and useful, part of a team working for a common goal. Dan's parishioners were warm, kind and loyal. Their absolute acceptance of Nathan as one of their own only heightened his longing for his own parish. Did he dare even hope for such a thing?

He paused, watching the men nailing plywood over the broken window, and waited for the familiar pain and guilt to swamp him.

But it didn't.

Dan came up behind him. "The girls have food ready. Why don't you take a break?"

Nathan gave him a weary smile. "Only if you join me."

Dan returned the smile. "I wouldn't miss Gwen's chili for anything."

As they walked toward the rectory, Dan turned serious. "I can't tell you how much I appreciate your help today, Nathan."

"Don't mention it. You'd have done the same."

Dan nodded. "Times like this make you appreciate your friends and your community."

"They sure do." Nathan gave Dan a pensive look as they mounted the stairs to the house. "I'd like to set up a date to talk to you again whenever you can manage it." He stopped. "Sorry. Timing's probably not the best."

A grin spread across Dan's boyish face. "No time like the present. I'll check my schedule as soon as we eat."

Chapter Twelve

On her way through the Wyndermere lobby the next day, Paige picked up a newspaper from the front desk counter, pausing to scan the headlines. According to national weather reports, a small tornado had indeed passed by yesterday, touching down briefly in a wooded area to the north of them. Thankfully the only damage sustained was some fallen trees and a few downed power lines. Wyndermere itself had come through relatively unscathed with some minor water damage and a few uprooted trees on the property.

That morning, Paige and Sandy had kept the children's schedule running as close to normal as possible, while Jerry helped the rest of the crew with the outdoor cleanup. She looked at her watch as she walked. Hopefully the work was finished by now. They needed Jerry for the last rehearsal before the play's grand performance tomorrow.

Paige's pulse skittered as her thoughts turned to Nathan. If he followed his usual routine, he'd probably come to watch them rehearse. After the intimate moments spent together yesterday, the way he'd bandaged her hands and held her during the ordeal, Paige wasn't sure how to react around him. The feelings she'd been trying so hard to ignore kept bubbling to the surface.

Tucking the folded newspaper under her arm with her clipboard, she pushed through the auditorium doors. Right away, her gaze collided with Nathan's across the room. He moved away from the stage and headed toward her. She swallowed her nerves and pasted on a smile.

"How are you this morning?" His gaze was warm and friendly.

She moved the clipboard, hugging it to her torso, as if shielding herself from her emotions. "Okay. And you?"

He smiled, rubbing his upper arm. "Muscles are sore. Haven't done that much manual labor in a while."

She shifted in her sneakers. "I wanted to thank you for... well, for everything." She willed the color from creeping into her cheeks.

He glanced at the bandages still covering her hands. "Someone had to look after you. Did George speak to you yet?"

She frowned. "How did you know?"

A light of amusement shone in his eyes. "I figured he'd have a few choice things to say."

She lifted her chin. "You may be surprised to learn that he thanked me for helping."

"Really?" He raised a brow. "I thought he'd chew you out for disobeying orders."

She let out a sigh. "That, too. The truth is I deserved a reprimand. Being impulsive is one of my biggest flaws."

"And one of your more charming features." He winked at her, and Paige's heart skipped into overdrive.

The sound of children's voices pulled her back into work mode. "I'd love to stay and discuss my charms, but I'm late for rehearsal."

His low chuckle rumbled behind her as she hurried to meet the campers.

Two hours and several small mishaps later, they wrapped up the dress rehearsal. Overall, Paige was pleased with the performance. She jotted ideas on her clipboard for a few subtle changes that would make things run more smoothly.

As she passed through the hall on her way to the change room, she found Jerry sprawled on a bench, eyes closed.

She gave his shoulder a playful punch. "Hey, why so gloomy? Everything went great."

When he opened his eyes, alarm shot through her. His face was chalky white, his eyes glassy.

"You don't look so good."

He wiped the sweat from his brow. "Just tired."

"You must have overdone it yesterday." She peered closer. "Are you sure you're not coming down with something?"

He shrugged off her concern and got to his feet. "Nah. It's this costume and the stage lights. I'll be fine."

She frowned. "If you say so."

Despite his assurances, an uneasy feeling plagued Paige as she watched him leave.

The next morning it was official. Jerry had contracted a nasty stomach virus and would be unable to perform in the play.

Paige sat in the cafeteria, her breakfast untouched, trying to imagine how she was going to break the news to the kids. In addition, she now had to juggle their schedule for the day's activities without Jerry.

Equally dejected, Sandy picked at her eggs. "What a shame after all their hard work."

"They're going to be so disappointed." Paige sighed. "Maybe we can do the play at the end of August, instead of the talent show I had planned."

"Maybe."

Paige pulled out her clipboard and pen. "Right now we need to change today's activities."

The two were deep in concentration over the paperwork when a shadow fell across the table. Paige glanced up, surprised to see Nathan standing there, looking crisp and neat in dark pants and a white golf shirt.

"Good morning, ladies. I hear you have a dilemma on your hands."

Paige frowned. "How did you know? We haven't told anyone yet."

"I ran into George in the dining room. He told me about Jerry."

Sandy drained the last of her orange juice and stood to leave.

"Wait a minute, please," Nathan said. "I have a proposition for you both."

Sandy folded her arms and cocked her head to one side. "What kind of proposition?"

Nathan looked from one woman to the other. "What would you think of me playing the part of the captain?"

Paige's jaw dropped open, but no words formed. Nathan as the male lead—opposite her?

"I've been at almost all the rehearsals, and I've played the part before. I'm sure if I run over the script a few times today, I could manage it."

"No." Panic snaked through Paige's chest. *Not a good idea.* Not when it would mean having to *kiss* at the end.

Sandy frowned. "Why not? I think it's a fantastic idea."

Paige's mind reeled, her gaze fused to the papers on the table. "A different captain will throw the kids off. And the costume won't fit."

Sandy's dark eyes narrowed. "The kids will adapt. And I can fix the costume this afternoon."

Paige searched for a valid reason to refuse and couldn't come up with a thing. "I don't know. This could be a disaster." Especially for her. A kiss would do nothing to help diminish her attraction to Nathan.

Nathan studied her. "We don't want to let the kids down,

do we? A mediocre performance would be better than none at all."

"I agree." Sandy shot to her feet, tugging Paige's arm. "Come on. We've got a lot of work to do. Nathan, I'll meet you later to adjust the costume."

Paige rose, her jaw tight. "I guess it's settled then."

If only her stomach would settle, as well.

Paige was too busy all day to worry about the play. By the time dinner hour rolled around, a mixture of nerves and excitement made it impossible for the kids to eat. Paige tried her best to subdue their nervous energy as well as control her own unusual case of butterflies.

Finally the time arrived to get into costume. Paige left Sandy in charge of the kids while she went to change. Alone in her dressing area, she bowed her head to pray.

"Lord, we need Your help tonight. Guide us to give the best performance we can in Your name." She paused. *"And please help me get through this. Protect my heart and keep this strictly professional. Amen."*

As usual, praying restored her equilibrium, allowing her to remember that God was in charge, and that He'd help her through this challenge. She changed into her costume, pinned up her hair and applied her makeup. Once satisfied, she stepped out from behind the curtain and slammed straight into Nathan.

She gasped as he reached out to steady her.

"Sorry. I was coming to tell you to break a leg."

"Oh."

She took a step back to look at him, and her breath tangled in her lungs. *Magnificent* was the only word that registered in her brain. In the full captain's uniform, he cut an incredibly handsome figure.

She swallowed. "You look wonderful. Sandy did a great job."

"That she did." He frowned. "Are you okay?"

"Just nervous, I guess."

He gave her arm a light squeeze. "Relax. Everything will go smoothly."

She nodded and tried to smile. "I hope so. See you onstage."

She hurried over to check on the kids, glad he didn't know that *he* made her more nervous than the upcoming performance.

After the first few minutes of the play, Paige settled into the familiarity of her role and allowed herself to relax. Nathan performed his part to perfection. Paige was pleasantly surprised by his transformation into his character and by his rich baritone voice. If she were honest, he made a far better captain than Jerry.

At the last costume change, Paige hurried backstage to pull on the gauzy dress she would wear during her duet with Nathan. As she brushed out her hair, she concentrated on rehearsing the song in her head, imagining how well their voices would blend, firmly blocking out the image of the kiss at the end of the scene.

Her traitorous heart, however, pumped out a wild rhythm the moment Nathan joined her onstage. He reached out to take her hands as they began their duet. Just as Paige had imagined, the combination of her soprano and his deep baritone blended in perfect harmony. They stood a whisper apart, hands joined as they sang. Caught up in her character's emotion, Paige stared into the swirling depths of Nathan's vivid eyes. Why was it so easy to pretend the emotion shining there was really meant for her? As the song drew to a close, her heart raced, half in dread, half in anticipation. Her eyes fluttered closed, her face tilted upward, until she felt the warmth of his lips on hers.

Electricity raced through her system as reality and fiction blurred together. Her lips parted and the kiss deepened.

She became aware of the hush surrounding them, the scent of his cologne, the smooth fabric of his uniform beneath her palm. Time stilled, until the sound of applause brought reality crashing in on her. On the outskirts of her consciousness, she became aware that the curtain had come down and that she and Nathan stood alone on the darkened stage. Heat flooded her cheeks, and she jerked out of his arms.

"I—I have to go," she stammered, walking backward, eyes locked with his.

Finally turning, she ran from the stage, not daring to look back.

Somehow Paige made it through the rest of the play on autopilot. A standing ovation greeted them at the end of the last scene. Nathan held her hand as they took a bow, and Zach came forward with an armful of red roses for her. Paige kissed Zach on the cheek and curtsied once more before the final curtain fell.

"Great job, everyone," she told the kids, who were giving high fives all around. "After you've changed, we'll meet in the cafeteria for cake and punch."

Whoops of delight followed as they filed off the stage. In the ensuing silence, she forced herself to turn and face Nathan, who stood waiting behind her.

"Thank you so much for filling in. You did an amazing job." She hoped her voice sounded somewhere near normal.

His eyes were unreadable as he watched her. "And you were wonderful, as always."

Did she imagine an extra layer of meaning to his words? She managed a smile. "Thanks. I'd better go change."

He snagged her hand before she could get away. "Why bother? You look beautiful in that dress."

Her pulse picked up speed despite her best efforts to remain unmoved.

Before she could answer, Sandy appeared. "Come on, you two. Everyone's waiting for the stars of the show."

"Ready?" Nathan asked, not releasing her hand.

She nodded, finding it near impossible to pull her gaze from his.

"Good."

She tried to disengage her hand, but he linked his fingers through hers. Panic rose inside her. She sent Sandy a desperate look, silently begging for help, but her friend only grinned.

Fat lot of help she is.

Once in the crowded cafeteria, Paige was able to put some distance between herself and Nathan, though she felt his eyes on her the whole time. Her emotions were in turmoil. She longed to escape, to be alone to sort through her feelings and gain some perspective. She couldn't do that under Nathan's intense scrutiny.

Half an hour later, Paige rounded up the kids to say their good-nights and, with Sandy's help, herded them back to the cabins. A sense of relief invaded her tense muscles when she managed to get away without being cornered by Nathan—a slight reprieve until the morning, when she hoped her world would return to normal.

It took a concentrated effort to get the children settled into bed. Once calmness reigned again, Paige moved into her area of the cabin and pulled the privacy curtain closed. Though certain she was far too keyed up to sleep, she changed into cotton pajamas.

Sandy slipped through the curtain a few minutes later. Paige stopped folding her clothes to glance over at her friend, who stood staring with her arms crossed.

"What's wrong? Is Jerry okay?" Sandy had gone to check on him once the girls were settled.

"He's doing better. He'll need another day or two to recuperate though. George is staying in the cabin with the boys for now."

Unable to bear her sharp gaze, Paige turned back to the rickety dresser and tugged open a drawer. "We'll just have to work around Jerry's absence, like we did today."

Sandy plopped down on Paige's bed. "So what's the deal with you and Nathan Porter?"

Paige stilled, though her heart ricocheted against her ribcage. "I have no idea what you're talking about."

"You don't?" Disbelief tinged Sandy's voice.

Paige closed the drawer with a thunk. "No, I don't." Neutral expression in place, she turned to face her friend.

"Then what was that kiss all about?" Sandy demanded.

Telltale warmth crept into Paige cheeks. "It was scripted. You know that." *If she denied it long enough, maybe they could both believe it.*

Sandy snorted and crossed her legs on the bed. "Come on, Paige. That was one intense kiss."

Paige's shoulders slumped. She sank to the bed and dropped her head into her hands. "Was it that obvious?"

"Only to anyone who knows you well."

Paige groaned. "Which means half of Wyndermere is talking about it."

Sandy put a comforting arm around her shoulders. "Don't worry about that. I just want to know what's going on with you."

Paige fought back sudden tears that stung her eyes. "I'm so confused," she whispered. "I don't want to be attracted to him."

"Oh, honey." Sandy hugged her close. "Why not?"

Paige shook her head. "Losing Colin almost killed me. I made a vow I would never let myself be that vulnerable again."

"Is it so terrible to be interested in someone?" Sandy

asked. "From what I can tell, he feels the same way about you."

A tear escaped to slip down Paige's cheek. "I feel like I'm betraying Colin's memory, betraying our love."

Sandy squeezed her arm. "It's been four years," she said gently. "Don't you think it's time?"

Paige swiped at the tears and got up to pace the room on shaky legs. When she didn't answer the question, Sandy came to stand in front of her. She laid warm hands on Paige's shoulders.

"Would Colin want you to spend the rest of your life alone? With no husband, no family?"

A sigh rasped out. "Probably not."

"He'd want you to find someone else…and be happy."

Paige shook her head, her heart heavy with an all-consuming sadness. "I don't think I can do that, Sandy. I'm just not brave enough."

Nathan stood at the inn's railing, inhaling the cool evening air, trying to come to grips with the roller coaster of emotions he'd experienced over the course of the night. He indulged himself for a moment, reliving the duet he'd performed with Paige. It had been amazing, the way she'd looked into his eyes as she sang. Something special had passed between them, culminating in that soul-searing kiss. Her sweet response had made him forget all about the audience, as though they were the sole inhabitants of the universe. Sensations unlike anything he'd ever experienced before had raced through his body.

Nathan could no longer deny the truth. Without intending to, he'd come to develop strong feelings for Paige. Feelings that were becoming harder and harder to ignore.

Footsteps rang out on the stone terrace, jarring him out of his thoughts. George moved up beside him to stare out over the dark water.

"Great job tonight, Nate. Didn't know you were so talented."

Nathan chuckled. "Thanks. It was fun to sing again." It *had* been enjoyable. The first time in more than a year that he'd done something for pure pleasure. Seeing the kids, Zach especially, so proud of themselves, basking in their parents' applause, made everything worthwhile.

George cleared his throat. "You and Paige seemed pretty...chummy up there. Anything I should know?"

Nathan shifted his weight. "Are you asking as her employer or as my friend?"

The weight of George's stare forced Nathan to look at him. "Does it matter?"

"It might."

"As your friend then. Keeping in mind that I'm Paige's friend, too."

Nathan didn't miss the hint of steel in George's tone. He released a quiet sigh. "It's complicated, George. I can't deny I have feelings for her. What that means, I don't know."

"What does Paige feel?"

Nathan expelled a long breath. "I have no idea." She'd responded to his kiss, no doubt about that. But did that mean she cared for him?

George shot him a dubious glance. "Just a word of caution. Be careful with her. Paige is a lot more fragile than she looks."

"I'll keep that in mind."

George's pager buzzed and he snatched it up. "Sorry. I'm needed." He shot Nathan a serious look. "I meant what I said, Nate. I won't stand by and see Paige hurt."

After George left, Nathan lowered himself to sit on the stone wall. Part of him bristled at the implied warning George had given him, part of him completely understood the protective instincts Paige brought out in George—because he felt them, too.

No matter which way Nathan looked at it, tonight had changed the dynamics of his relationship with Paige. Feelings had been awakened that could no longer be repressed. But was he ready to explore them, to see where they might lead? He just wasn't sure. And what about Paige? What did she want?

Tomorrow, he promised himself. Tomorrow he would talk to her and get the answers he needed.

For tonight, he would be content with the memory of his lips on hers.

The next afternoon, Paige closed the door to her office with a sigh and flipped on the light. It was her first chance all day to just breathe. The weather had turned wet after lunch, so she left Sandy to supervise the kids in the auditorium, while Paige finished her paperwork. She'd been putting off applying for more financial aid, but time was quickly running out.

She crossed to the credenza and plugged in her kettle. When the door opened behind her, she frowned, frustration humming through her veins. "I'm not in the mood, Sandy."

Every chance she got, Sandy had been pleading the cause of true love, trying to convince Paige of something she knew could never be.

"Not in the mood for what?"

Her hand froze at the sound of Nathan's voice. She lowered her cup to the desktop and then, steeling herself, she turned to face him.

"Hello, Nathan."

He loomed larger than life in the doorway for a moment, before closing the door with a sharp click. Paige started, feeling like a mouse caught in a trap.

"I'd like a word with you, if you don't mind."

She tried to swallow but found her mouth too dry. "Actually, I'm pretty busy—"

"This won't take long."

The tone of his voice broached no argument. That, along with the intensity in his eyes, made nerves skitter down her spine. "Fine."

He stepped toward her. "I wanted to talk to you about the play yesterday."

"Oh?" Hiding behind the silky shield of her hair, she jumped when Nathan tipped her chin up, forcing her to look at him.

"I want an honest answer to my question."

She could only stare, her heart thrumming against her ribs at his nearness.

"Did you feel something incredible when we kissed last night?"

Her pulse raced so fast the room spun around her. She couldn't let him guess how that kiss had affected her. Instead, she pulled every scrap of pride around her like a protective suit of armor. "It was a stage kiss, Nathan."

"Really? That's all?"

"Yes." She tried to shift past him, but he took a step to the side and blocked her path.

"That's funny," he said, "because I've never experienced a kiss like that—onstage or otherwise."

She took a step back for sheer self-preservation. He only closed the gap. The proverbial mousetrap clamped shut.

She lifted her chin. "You imagined it."

"I don't think so." He moved closer still, so close that she could feel the warmth of his breath when he asked, "Why are you fighting your feelings?"

She sank against the wall, knees shaking. "Because I can't betray Colin's memory like this."

He jerked as if she'd slapped him.

"I'm sorry, Nathan," she whispered. "I can't do this."

Raw pain shone in his eyes as he stared, unmoving. Seconds ticked by until he finally took a deliberate step away from her. "If that's your decision, then I'll respect your wishes. I won't mention it again."

When the door clicked shut behind him with a foreboding sense of finality, Paige closed her eyes and bit back a sob.

She'd broken every rule in the book by getting emotionally involved with the parent of a patient. How could she have let this happen?

She sagged against her desk, disgust twisting her insides into knots. The fact that she'd secretly wanted Nathan to kiss her again had paralyzed her with fear, proving she'd been right to reject him.

With no guarantee that she would ever be able to open her heart to love again, giving Nathan false hope would be the cruelest thing she could do. Better to push him away now—before she hurt him even worse in the future.

Chapter Thirteen

Three days later, Paige sat on the end of the dock, her bare toes skimming the surface of the water. Despite the beauty of the sun glistening on the blue-glass lake, she couldn't shake the depression that had plagued her ever since her *encounter* with Nathan. Though her head knew she'd done the right thing, her heart refused to concede the wisdom of her actions.

Nathan had avoided her ever since. She missed his comforting presence, his smile and the way her pulse kicked up a notch when he came in the room. It scared her how much she'd come to crave his company in such a short amount of time—how easily he'd wormed his way past her defenses.

Today she'd decided to quit wallowing in her misery and get on with things. Since Nathan hadn't rescinded her services, she still owed it to Zach to finish his sessions. A true professional would put all personal feelings aside and concentrate on the patient. She reminded herself of this as she waited for Zach to arrive. The sound of the boy's laughter broke through her thoughts. She straightened and attempted to push back the melancholy before he joined her. The wooden boards soon vibrated with the pounding of Zach and Goliath racing up the dock.

"Hi, Paige." The boy plunked down beside her and pulled the dog along with him, looping his arm around the beast's neck.

"Hi, Zach. Are you finished walking Goliath?"

"Yeah. I'll take him home after we're done."

"Sounds good." She rubbed the dog's big head, and allowed herself the comfort of Goliath's shaggy presence, while mentally switching into therapy mode.

She took two sodas from the small cooler beside her and handed one to Zach. "So how are things between you and your dad lately?"

He popped the tab and took a sip. "Okay. I think he likes me better now."

Paige let the comment slide and waited for more.

"He's not so mad, and he doesn't yell as much." Zach paused. "Except after the play, he got real grumpy again."

Paige inwardly cringed. She hated being the cause of any more pain for Nathan and Zach.

Goliath grunted and plopped his head down on his paws, as if protesting Zach's lack of attention.

Zach fiddled with the tab on his can. "Do you think he's mad at me?"

The vulnerability in his voice caused a fresh wave of guilt. She could no longer deny the truth. She'd broken protocol and become overly invested in her patient and his father. Had her unprofessionalism sent them backward in their recovery?

She sighed. "Zach, your dad's not mad at you. He's mad at me. We had a…disagreement after the play."

Zach eyed her with open curiosity. "What about?"

She shrugged, pushing away the memory of Nathan's ravaged eyes. "Grown-up stuff. Nothing for you to worry about." She reached into the cooler and pulled out a container of grapes.

"Can I ask you something?" Zach swung his legs, his sneaker thumping against the wooden leg of the dock.

"I'm the one who's supposed to be asking you questions, remember?"

He scrunched up his nose. "If I answer your questions, will you answer mine?"

Paige thought for a minute while she chewed. "I guess that's fair, but I get to go first." Maybe she could distract him so he'd forget what he wanted to ask. "Have you forgiven your dad for not letting you and your mom come back home?" She handed him the fruit.

"I think so. You helped me understand why he couldn't do it." He popped a grape into his mouth.

"I'm glad. Being able to forgive is a big thing."

He shrugged. "My turn for a question."

"Okay. Shoot."

He squinted at her. "Do you like my dad?"

She hesitated, sensing an underlying meaning to the question. "Of course, I do. Your dad's a nice man."

"I mean, as a boyfriend?"

A trickle of perspiration slid down her spine as she fought to keep her expression neutral. How did she answer that without blatantly lying? "I'm not looking for a boyfriend, honey," she said gently, forcing her thoughts away from the memory of Nathan's lips on hers. "Let's get back to you."

Zach frowned, clearly unhappy with her response.

She paused, hoping her next question wouldn't be too difficult. Instinctively she softened her voice. "Would you like to tell me a bit about your mom now?"

At first he shook his head, his face partly hidden by the brim of his red ball cap. Then he looked up at her with sad eyes. "Could I?"

"Sure."

"My dad doesn't like to talk about her."

"Talking about someone who died is sometimes too painful. But I think it helps us remember them in a good way."

He nodded, picking at a knot in the wood. "My mom

was real pretty. Kinda skinny with long brown hair and blue eyes. She used to be sad sometimes. But other times she'd play with me and laugh a lot. She had a nice laugh."

"She sounds like a good mom. What was your favorite thing to do together?"

He smiled, but his eyes remained sad. "We went bike riding a lot. Dad was always busy at work, so it was just me and Mom. Sometimes she let my friend come with us."

They sat in silence for a while, with nothing but the soft lap of water against the dock, until Zach broke the stillness. "Paige, why do you think God made my mom get sick?"

The question was one she'd asked a million times when Colin died. Now, after all her reflections on the subject, the words sat right there waiting to be said. "God didn't make her get sick, honey. Bad things just happen sometimes. God is there to help us get through them."

"Did He help you when your boyfriend died?"

"Yes, He did. I still miss Colin, but now I can enjoy remembering the happy times. That will happen for you, too, eventually."

Zach crinkled his nose. "Don't you ever want another boyfriend?"

A wave of sadness pinched her heart. "I don't know. But right now, I'm just not ready."

He stared at her with wise eyes and nodded. "Maybe someday I'll be ready for a new mom, too."

Nathan paced Dan Redding's office, waiting for him to finish a call. The cozy office with bookcases along one wall and a large sunny window on the other did little to improve his mood. He paused to read some framed inspirational quotes on the wall—anything to keep from thinking about the sting of Paige's rejection.

"Sorry about that," Dan apologized as he hung up.

"No problem." Nathan reclaimed his seat.

"You were telling me about the guilt you felt whenever you were called away from your family."

Nathan nodded and steepled his fingers together, trying to focus back on the previous conversation. "Yes. Cynthia always made me feel terrible for leaving, no matter how valid the reason. And after a fight with her, I never felt I was giving one hundred percent to the person I was supposed to be helping."

"That must have made your job very difficult."

"It did. Things got even worse when Cynthia stopped coming to church altogether."

Dan shook his head. "I can't imagine it."

Nathan rubbed his hands over his eyes. "I felt like such a failure, like the world's biggest hypocrite. I couldn't function as a pastor. Couldn't preach love and forgiveness when I was filled with rage."

Dan let the words sit for a moment. "I'm sure if you had explained the situation, your parishioners would have understood. You're not the first minister to have his marriage fail."

"Maybe." Nathan sighed. He'd been too mired in bitterness and shame to think along those lines. Too mortified by the fact that his wife had betrayed him and moved in with another man.

"How did they respond when Cynthia died?"

He shrugged. "They were wonderful, of course. Came to the funeral. Brought a ton of food, most of which is still in my freezer."

"They wanted to show their love and support."

Nathan shook his head. "But I didn't deserve it. I was responsible for Cynthia's death. When I wouldn't take her back, we had a huge fight. The stress caused her aneurysm."

Dan took a deep breath and let it out slowly. "Nathan, that simply is not true." He held up a hand to ward off the argument that sprang to Nathan's lips. "A good friend of mine died the same way. Dropped dead in his garage, fixing his truck. The doctor told his wife it could've happened anytime, anywhere. The circumstances had nothing whatsoever to do with it."

A glimmer of hope sparked in Nathan. "A doctor said this?"

"Yes. Apparently his wife felt terrible because she'd yelled at him right before he went out to the garage. She got three different doctors to tell her the same thing before she finally let go of the guilt."

Untold emotions raced through Nathan's system. Did he dare believe what Dan was telling him?

"You have a lot to reflect on and pray about," Dan said. "Why don't we meet again tomorrow or the next day? In the meantime, I want you to think about the possibility of going back to New York to get some closure. Maybe that will help you decide whether you can return to your ministry there, or if you should make a clean break and start over in a new parish." He paused. "You need to consider that God could be leading you in a new direction."

Somewhat stunned, Nathan nodded and rose to shake Dan's hand.

After he left, Nathan drove for thirty minutes without realizing where he was headed. His mind swirled with thoughts and emotions, and driving helped him think.

Dan's words had given him a faint glimmer of hope. Maybe, just maybe, he hadn't caused Cynthia's aneurysm after all. Maybe he could finally let go of his guilt. He planned on talking to a few doctors himself to get a consensus of opinion—something he should have done long ago instead of taking the words of one person to heart. Though back then he hadn't been ready to hear the truth, no matter who told him.

His thoughts turned to his career as he steered the car back toward Wyndermere. Dan was right about needing closure. No matter what he decided about his future, he would have to go back, even if only to say goodbye. He sighed. The knot in his stomach told him he needed more time to work up the courage for that.

As the car slid down the highway, he couldn't help but think of Paige, the woman he'd come to feel so strongly about. Without her, he wouldn't have made such progress toward healing. Somehow she'd known Dan could help him. And her work with Zach was yielding slow but steady results. He had so many reasons to be grateful to her...yet the hurt he felt at her rejection overshadowed everything else. Had she allowed him to explain, he would have told her that he was uncertain, too—that he shared her doubts and fears about falling in love again, but that he wanted the chance to see where the powerful attraction between them could lead. But she had not been willing to even hear him out. And now even the friendship they'd been building seemed to have disappeared.

His fingers tightened on the wheel as he drove down the winding road leading to the inn. She'd been avoiding him ever since the confrontation in her office, and he had to admit, he'd been avoiding her, too. Because every time he saw her, he wanted to kiss her again.

Pulling into the designated parking area, he turned off the engine and got out of the car. His shoulders bowed with the weight of his remorse. He owed her a huge apology for forcing the issue.

Looking at his watch, he made up his mind. At this time of day, she usually worked in her office. Maybe if he apologized, they could get back to at least being friends.

For Zach's sake, he had to try.

The phone in her office rang as Paige filed the last piece of paper. At the sound of her brother's voice, a smile bloomed.

"Hey, Matt. I was going to call Mom and Dad later today. I can't wait to see you guys this weekend." She'd been looking forward to her brother's birthday party all week, hoping that a visit with her family would restore her good spirits.

Her smile faded at the silence on the other end.

"I'm sorry, Paige. I'm phoning with bad news."

Icy fingers of fear wound their way up her spine. The receiver weighed like lead in her hand. "What's wrong, Matti?"

"It's Dad." A long pause followed, giving Paige time to imagine all kinds of horrible possibilities.

"He's had a heart attack."

"No," Paige gasped. It wasn't possible. Her father worked out at the gym on a regular basis and was in great shape for his age. "How…how bad is it?"

"We don't know yet. The doctors are with him now."

Paige became aware of hospital noises in the background.

"He may need surgery, if he's strong enough." Matt's voice cracked. "You'd better come home, Paige."

Shock reverberated through her body, as her mind struggled to grasp the fact that her father may be dying. "I'll leave right away. Tell Daddy I'm coming."

She hung up the phone with shaking hands and closed her eyes.

Please, God, don't let my father die. I couldn't bear it. Not again.

As Nathan approached Paige's office, he steeled himself for his apology. He knocked once and waited. When there was no response, he pushed the door open and peered inside.

"Paige?"

She sat with her head in her hands, her eyes closed.

Alarm seeped through him. "Is everything all right?" He pushed farther into the room.

Slowly she lifted her head, a startled expression on her face. "Nathan. What are you doing here?"

"I wanted to talk to you, but if this is a bad time—"

Her gaze bounced around the room. "Actually it is. I have to leave." She shuffled some items on her desk, eyes unfocused.

Nathan frowned. "Where are you going?"

"Home." Her voice cracked with emotion.

Then he noticed her ashen skin, her shaking hands. Anxiety filled him as he approached her. "What's the matter?"

She bit down on her quivering lip. "My father had a heart attack."

The suddenness of her statement hit him like a splash of cold lake water. "I'm so sorry. Is he going to be okay?"

"I don't know. That's why I have to get home." She flipped open her laptop and started tapping away at the keys.

Nathan stuffed his hands into his pockets, helpless concern roaring through him as she madly clicked the mouse. He wished he could offer her some form of comfort, like a hug, but that was impossible right now. "What are you looking for?"

"The number for the bus station."

He reached out to capture her cold, trembling hands in his. "You don't need that. I'll take you."

Her eyes flew up to his. "I can't let you do that. It's a nine-hour drive."

"And a lot longer by bus."

She tried to pull her hands away, but he held them fast. "I'll rent a car then." Desperation laced her words.

He would never let her set off by herself in this state of shock. "You're too upset to drive." He kept his tone soothing, hoping to calm her agitation. "Please let me do this. I have the car and the time. Maybe it will help make up for my bad behavior the other day."

She hesitated, a storm of turmoil evident in her eyes. "What about Zach? He'll feel abandoned if we both leave."

"I'll give him the option of coming with us."

She sagged then, as though the energy had drained out of her. Nathan fought the overwhelming urge to pull her close, to protect her from everything bad in the world.

Instead he gave her hand a final squeeze. "We're wasting time. Go get your things and meet me at the car."

Chapter Fourteen

The scenery flew past the car window in a blur. Paige stared without focusing and lifted silent prayers for her dad, while trying to comprehend how this had all come about. How she'd ended up in Nathan's car on her way to see her father, who could be slipping away as they drove. The whole situation was beyond surreal.

She laid her head back and closed her eyes. On top of being worried sick, her senses screamed at being confined in this cramped space with Nathan mere inches away—so strong and solid that all she wanted to do was rest her head on his shoulder, let him hold her and tell her everything would be all right.

The ball of fear in the pit of her stomach reminded her why that wasn't possible.

She was thankful for Zach's presence in the backseat, just in case temptation overtook good sense.

Three hours into the trip, Nathan stopped to refuel and pick up some burgers and sodas. Paige didn't think she could eat a thing, but Nathan persuaded her to take a few bites. Zach happily finished the rest.

"I'm sorry your dad's sick," Zach told her after he'd finished eating. "Are you scared?"

She nodded, blinking to hold back the tears that threatened. "Very scared."

Zach reached between the seats to take her hand in his sticky one, almost undoing her carefully held control.

"Remember what you told me? That God always helps us get through the bad things? God will help you, too, Paige."

"Thank you, Zach." Her voice was a whisper as she blinked again, overcome by the compassion in this wonderful boy. Whatever mistakes Cynthia had made in her life, she'd succeeded in raising one terrific son.

As the trip progressed, Paige tried to sleep, but couldn't get comfortable against the headrest. In the dark of the night, the only thing visible outside the window was the glare of the oncoming headlights. Restless, she pulled out her cell phone and dialed her mother's number. The call went straight to voice mail. Paige left a brief message telling her she was halfway there, and then tried her brother's cell. When she got no answer, she tossed the phone back into her bag and crossed her arms with a sigh. Why weren't they answering? Had her dad's condition deteriorated? She squeezed her eyes shut, trying to will the terrifying thoughts away.

Some time later, a change in the speed of the car had Paige sitting upright and rubbing her eyes. She must have dozed off at last. She blinked to focus. Nathan had pulled into a truck stop.

"Sorry," he said. "Need a coffee."

Remorse set in when she noticed the fatigue around his eyes. "Do you want me to drive for a while?"

He unhooked his seat belt. "I'll be fine after a jolt of caffeine."

He got out of the car before she could respond, then poked his head back in. "You want anything?"

"No, thanks." Caffeine was the last thing she needed.

While he was gone, she took the opportunity to undo her belt and stretch. She twisted around to look at Zach, who slept soundly in his booster seat, his head lolling against the side window. For a moment she envied his childlike ability to sleep no matter what. The fact that he was willing to give up a few days of camp life to come with them also touched her. Part of his motive was concern for her, she knew, but part of it was fear of being left behind by his father. At least Nathan acknowledged this fear and gave Zach's feelings the respect they deserved—evidence of the changes he'd made to help his son.

She turned back to see Nathan arriving with his coffee.

He got in and handed her a bottle of water. "How are you holding up?"

She shrugged. "I'm not sure."

He started the engine, and then paused with his hand on the gearshift. "I'm praying for your father."

Knowing how Nathan had been struggling with his prayer life, that simple statement warmed her heart. "Thank you. That means a lot."

He pulled out of the rest area and slid the car back onto the highway. "I should be thanking you for all you've done. Zach is improving, and my talks with Dan are really helping. Because of you, I think we're going to get through this ordeal."

"I'm glad," she said, and meant it. But why did it make her sad to think of the time when Zach and Nathan would no longer need her?

The clock read 1:15 a.m. when Nathan pulled into Mercy Hospital in Portsmouth, New Jersey. He parked the car, then roused Paige and Zach from sleep. Paige stretched and pushed the hair off her face. He could tell by her frown the moment she remembered where they were—and why.

"We'll come in with you," Nathan said, "then play it by ear from there."

She nodded and gave him a tremulous smile. Was it his imagination or did she seem grateful for his presence?

At the information desk, a stout nurse told them Dave McFarlane was on the fourth floor and directed them to the elevators. When the doors opened at their destination, Paige burst out like a racehorse from the starting gate. She looked left and right, then rushed down the corridor straight into the arms of a tall man with shaggy blond hair. Holding Zach's hand, Nathan watched the man bury his face in her hair, and a stab of jealousy ripped through him. Seconds later, he realized it must be her brother. He expelled a breath and started down the hall toward them. A plump woman, not much taller than Paige, joined the pair, enveloping them both in a warm embrace.

Nathan held back, giving the family time to reconnect and get their bearings. He caught a glimpse of tears on Paige's face, and his heart twisted. With every fiber of his being, he prayed they weren't too late for her to see her father. Paige wiped her face, turned and caught his eye, motioning for them to come forward.

"Nathan and Zach," she said, "this is my mother, Donna, and my brother, Matt."

Donna looked to be in her midfifties. Her blond hair had faded, but her skin was clear and firm. He could see where Paige got her good features from. Matt, lanky and lean, shook his hand solemnly.

"I'm sorry to hear about your husband," Nathan said, turning back to Donna. "It must have been quite a shock."

"Yes, it was. Thank God we got him here in time."

"Dad's stable for the moment," Paige said. "I'm going in to see him."

Nathan smiled in relief. "That's good news. Zach and I will hang out in the waiting area until you're done."

Donna lingered behind until Matt and Paige had entered one of the rooms, then placed her hand on Nathan's arm.

"I want to thank you, Mr. Porter, for driving my daughter all this way."

"It was the least I could do. And please, call me Nathan."

She gave a weary smile. "Thank you, Nathan. You and your son must stay with us while you're here. I'll get Paige to give you directions to the house."

"Thank you. That's very kind."

After Donna left, Nathan and Zach waited in the lounge, watching late-night talk shows. When Paige finally came to find them, she looked exhausted but relieved.

"He's going to be okay. It was a relatively mild attack after all."

Nathan rose to cross the room. "That's great."

"They want to monitor him for a couple of days and run a few tests." She smoothed a hand over her hair, fiddling with the stray strands. Dark purple smudges stained the skin under her eyes.

She was ready to crash, Nathan surmised, both physically and emotionally. How could he get her to go home for some sleep?

"Your mother offered to let us stay at your house." He motioned over his shoulder to Zach lying across the seats. "I'd like to take Zach there, if you don't mind. You look like you could use some rest yourself."

Paige frowned. "I don't think—"

"That's a very good idea." Donna McFarlane entered the small room behind Paige.

"Mom, no," she cried, whirling around. "I don't want to leave Dad."

Donna put her hands on her daughter's shoulders. "Matt and I are here. And Dad's asleep now. He wouldn't want you to worry yourself sick. Go and get a couple hours of sleep."

Nathan knew Donna had won the moment Paige's shoulders sagged.

"All right. But call me if there's the slightest change."

* * *

Sleeping with Zach on a pullout couch in the McFarlanes' den proved interesting, although it didn't deter Nathan from getting several solid hours of rest. The clock read eight o'clock when he woke and made his way to the kitchen, where he found Zach and Paige sitting at the table, sharing a stack of pancakes. The aroma of fresh coffee filled the room. Nathan breathed in the scent appreciatively.

Paige looked up from her plate and smiled. "Good morning."

"Good morning. How are you feeling?"

"Much better. It's amazing what a little sleep can do." She scooped up her dirty dishes and rose. "Help yourself to the pancakes."

"They're awesome, Dad." Zach grinned, revealing a mouthful of half-eaten food.

"I'm sure they are." He sat down beside his son and picked up a plate.

"Would you like some coffee?" Paige looked fresh and pretty in a yellow top and jeans, her hair pulled back with some sort of scarf. Being back in her childhood home obviously agreed with her. She seemed more relaxed, more like herself.

"Definitely."

"How about I leave the whole pot on the table," she teased, bringing him a mug.

"One cup at a time will do, thank you." He took the mug from her with a smile. "How is your father this morning?"

"Better, according to Mom. I want to head over soon though, before they take him for more tests."

He nodded. "We'll leave as soon as we eat. After we drop you off, I thought Zach and I might take in a movie."

Zach's eyes widened, and a huge grin split his face. "Awesome. What can we see?"

"Your pick—as long as it's child appropriate." He winked at Zach and cut into his pancakes.

Zach bounced in his seat, enthusiasm oozing from every pore.

Paige, on the other hand, stood motionless by the kitchen sink. "I thought you might be heading back to Wyndermere today," she said quietly.

Nathan's hand stilled on his fork. Did she want him to leave? "We can stay as long as you need us."

"You're sure?"

"I'm sure."

Relief swept over her features, and he relaxed. It wasn't much, but at least she'd let him be there for her when she needed a friend.

Nathan pushed out the door of the diner, carrying a tray of burgers and fries. It was too perfect a day to eat indoors.

"Over here, Dad." Zach raced to the closest table shaded by a bright red umbrella.

Nathan chuckled as he followed the exuberant boy. Zach's enthusiasm made Nathan feel more alive than he had in months. He'd even enjoyed the animated Disney movie.

Nathan set the tray on the outdoor table and looped his legs over the bench to join Zach, who immediately plucked a fry from the container.

"Are we going back to the hospital after this?"

"We'll swing by and see how Paige is doing." Nathan unwrapped a burger and handed it to his son.

A frown wrinkled his forehead. "Is Paige's dad going to get better?"

"The doctors think so."

"I'm glad. I really like Paige, don't you?" Zach lifted the burger to his mouth, sauce oozing from the side.

"I do." Nathan shifted on his hard seat.

"She's pretty, too, don't you think?"

"Yes, she's pretty." Nathan reached over to dab a napkin at the dribble of mustard on Zach's chin.

"And you like kissing her, right?"

Nathan jerked his hand back as if scalded. "What?"

"You kissed her in the play."

"Zachary," he said, attempting to sound stern. "That was only acting."

The boy snorted. "It was a real kiss. I could tell."

Nathan's mind went blank. How did a seven-year-old become an expert on kissing?

"Are you going to marry her?"

"Nobody is getting married." The sharpness of his tone made Zach flinch. Nathan sighed and set aside his soda. "I'm sorry. I shouldn't have snapped at you."

"That's okay, Dad."

"The truth is," he said slowly, "I do like Paige, but she's not ready to date anyone yet. And to be honest, I'm not sure I am, either." He'd have liked to have had the chance to find out…but apparently it wasn't meant to be.

Zach's shoulders drooped. "I was hoping you could marry Paige, so I could have a new mom."

Nathan fought the rush of emotion in his chest and covered Zach's sticky hand with his own. "Maybe I'll get married again one day, but first you need time to get over missing your mom."

Zach looked up with eyes awash in sadness. "I miss her a lot. Do you?"

How could one simple question totally disarm him? For his son's sake, he tried to remember the happier times with Cynthia. "I'm very sad your mom died and that you won't get to see her again."

"Until Heaven," Zach corrected.

Nathan smiled. "Until Heaven."

Zach poked his straw into his cup. "You were mad at Mom, weren't you?"

Nathan fought the urge to vent his frustration. Instead he met Zach's gaze. His son deserved honesty. "For a long time I was. But now I understand why she left. None of our problems were your fault though. You know that, right?"

He gave a slight nod.

"Good. I don't want you to feel guilty."

Zach only shrugged, swirling the ice around and around in his cup.

"How would you feel about going back home for a day? I have to see some people at the church, and you could visit Grandpa and Grandma."

"Are you going back to work?"

Nathan sensed the fear behind the question. "I'm not sure yet. But no matter what I decide, things will be different this time. I plan to spend a lot more time with you. That's a promise."

His reward was Zach's huge smile. "I'd like that—a lot!"

"Good." Nathan gathered the trash onto the tray. "We'd better get back to the hospital."

He rose from the bench seat, stunned when Zach threw his arms around his waist in a tight embrace.

"I love you, Dad."

The dreaded lump returned, and Nathan swallowed hard. "I love you, too, Zach."

Chapter Fifteen

Dave's room was empty when Nathan and Zach returned to the hospital. Surely the tests were long over by now. Nathan went to inquire at the nurses' station. The young woman behind the desk shot him a sympathetic look.

"Oh, I'm sorry. Mr. McFarlane was taken into surgery several hours ago."

Nathan frowned. "He wasn't scheduled for surgery. Is he okay?" His stomach clenched, thinking of Paige. She would be devastated.

"I don't know. But you can go up to the next floor. The family is waiting there."

He grabbed Zach by the hand. "Thank you."

They found the McFarlanes seated in the surgical waiting room on the fifth floor. The women's red-rimmed eyes and Matt's grim expression told Nathan that Dave must have taken a serious turn for the worse. Paige looked up as they entered the room.

Nathan took a seat beside her, wishing he could do more to help. "A nurse said your father had been taken into surgery. What happened?"

Paige twisted a tissue in her hands until it shred beneath her fingers. "The tests showed three major blockages in his arteries. The doctors wanted to operate right away." She looked at her watch. "He's been in for three hours now."

"That must have been quite a shock."

"It was." Paige shifted in her chair, moving subtly away from him.

"Is there anything I can do?" Nathan asked. "Get you some coffee? Some food?"

"No, thanks." Paige leaned her head back against the wall and closed her eyes.

Nathan frowned, hating this return to her previous state of anxiety.

"Actually," Donna said, drawing his attention away from Paige, "I wouldn't mind a coffee and a muffin."

Nathan stood, relieved for something to do to combat his feeling of helplessness. "Sure. Matt, anything for you?"

The younger man shook his head. "Nothing, thanks."

Donna leaned forward and patted Paige's leg. "Honey, why don't you give Nathan a hand? You know what kind of muffins I like. Zach can stay here and we can get to know each other better."

Nathan marveled at Donna's inner fortitude. Her husband was having major surgery, and despite her own worries, she was trying to make sure everyone else was all right.

Despite Paige's protest, Nathan pulled her gently to her feet. "We'll be back in fifteen minutes."

Paige trudged down the hall beside Nathan, nursing resentment. What was her mother trying to do? Purposely push her toward Nathan?

"I know it's hard to look on the bright side right now," Nathan said, "but it's probably good the doctor acted so quickly instead of risking another heart attack."

She shrugged and pushed her hands deep into her pockets. "Two days ago my dad was perfectly healthy, or so we thought."

They turned a corner, heading toward the elevators,

when Nathan suddenly stopped in front of the door to the chapel.

"Would you like to go in for a minute?" he asked quietly.

She hesitated only a second, then nodded. She'd been here earlier in the day, but her dad could use as many prayers as possible. Nathan pushed the doors open into a small room and snapped on the light. Several rows of wooden benches sat before a plain white altar. A wooden cross hung on the wall above it.

Together they entered one of the pews. When she finished her prayer, Paige glanced over at Nathan. His eyes were closed, his head bowed over his entwined hands. Filled with a sudden yearning—for what, she wasn't sure—she forced her eyes back to the altar for another silent prayer, this time one of thanks for Nathan's returning faith.

"How was the movie?" she asked him later as they carried the coffee and muffins back upstairs.

"Surprisingly good. It made me realize what I've been missing. Spending time with Zach that way, I mean."

Paige smiled, happy to see Nathan making more of an effort to connect with his son. She knew it was a big part of the reason their relationship had taken such a positive turn.

As they neared the cardiac care unit, Paige put a hand on his arm. "Nathan, I want to thank you for everything."

He smiled. "You're welcome. I'm just glad I could help after everything you've done for us."

She paused, moistening her dry lips. "I won't be able to leave for at least two or three days—until I'm sure Dad's out of danger. You and Zach should probably head back to Wyndermere. I'll find a way back when I'm ready."

His eyes darkened as he studied her. She wished she knew what he was thinking. A secret part of her hoped he wouldn't leave, but the larger part feared he would stay.

She couldn't afford to become dependent on Nathan for her emotional well-being.

A nurse came toward them pushing a squeaky cart of medical supplies. Nathan moved to let her pass. "Actually I've been thinking of taking a side trip. Maybe Zach and I will do that and touch base with you when we're done."

Paige gave him a quizzical stare, her curiosity piqued. "A side trip where?"

An unreadable expression crossed his face. "Back home. It's time to face my past and make a decision about the future."

Her stomach lurched at his simple declaration. The reality that Nathan and Zach would soon return to their lives away from Wyndermere hit her hard. "Do you think you're ready?" she asked softly.

"I'm not sure. Guess I'll find out soon enough."

Driving back into his hometown past all the familiar landmarks, Nathan was unprepared for the onslaught of emotions that hit him. Unlike Zach, who seemed excited to be back, Nathan found the tension returning to his neck and shoulders, as well as a sickening sense of dread swirling in his stomach.

After dropping Zach off with his parents, who were delighted by the visit, Nathan drove over to Saint Stephen's church. He parked on the road in front of the red-bricked building and sat staring for a long time. Affection, fear and regret all warred to gain a foothold. At last he blew out a ragged breath and opened the car door. No point in stalling any longer.

With long strides he made his way up the sidewalk to the front door of the church, used his keys to open it and slipped inside. His eyes took a minute to adjust to the dim lighting. Familiar smells of polished wood and candle wax soothed him, bringing back the innate comfort he used to associate with the building. Gradually the muscles in his shoulders began to unclench. This was his church, his home—there was nothing to fear here.

When he reached the front, he bowed before the altar, then entered the first pew, raising his eyes to the cross on the wall. A wave of homesickness swept over him, a yearning for his former close relationship with his parishioners, now fractured by his long absence.

Lord, forgive me for letting them down. For letting You down. Please give me the courage to face the past and guide my decision for the future. Help me to do what's best for Zach, for me and for my parishioners. Amen.

Nathan expelled a loud breath and rose. His footsteps echoed on the tiled floor as he headed to the church offices. It seemed as if no time at all had passed when he fit the key into the lock, opened the door and flipped on the inside lights.

He stiffened then as the changes hit him full force. His temporary replacement, Reverend Pritchard, had completely rearranged the furniture and put up his own artwork. Nathan advanced farther into the room and stood behind the desk. His personal photos were gone, replaced with pictures of a man canoeing on a glass lake. Cautiously he moved around the desk to sit in the high-back chair. A group of cards was displayed on the desk, and Nathan couldn't help but read a few of the remarks inside.

"Dear Rev. Pritchard, Thank you for the wonderful sermon at my mother's funeral…"

"Thank you for your prayers for my daughter. God bless you, Rev. Pritchard."

His hand stilled as he read the last one.

"Dear Rev. Pritchard, Thanks for your help with the spring fund-raiser. This parish has come alive since you took over. I hope you will consider staying on permanently."

An invisible knife blade twisted Nathan's gut. With deliberate care, he placed the card back on the shelf. While he'd been stuck in the past, it seemed his parish had moved on without him. Nathan allowed the pain and disappointment to wash over him. He'd let his people down. They'd needed a spiritual leader to guide them, and he'd failed to fulfill his duties. Reverend Pritchard had stepped into his shoes and taken over—quite well apparently.

Nathan looked at his watch. It was almost time for his meeting with Bishop John Telford.

Footsteps in the hallway alerted Nathan to someone's approach. A tall, thin man appeared at his door in a charcoal-gray suit that complemented the silver in his hair.

"Bishop John," Nathan said, rising. "It's good to see you again."

The older man stepped inside and shook Nathan's hand warmly. "Good to see you, too, Nathan. You're looking well."

"Thank you. I'm feeling much better." He motioned for the bishop to take a seat. "I appreciate you rearranging your schedule to see me."

Bishop John nodded. "This meeting is long overdue and I didn't want to put it off." He crossed one leg over the other and leaned back. "So, Nathan, are you ready to come back to work?"

Nathan squirmed under John's serious gaze. He'd forgotten how direct his superior could be. No small talk to soften the way. "I'm still not sure if I can, John." His gaze roamed the room. "As much as I miss this place, there are too many bad memories here."

The disappointment in John's gray eyes made Nathan flinch.

"I'm sorry, too. The parish is losing a good man." John

nodded. "I'll put your name in for a new parish. Preferably one in this general area, I presume?"

Nathan's initial thoughts flew to Paige. He could ask for something that would put him closer to the college she attended. But he had to put Zach's needs first.

"Anything in this general area would be good. I'd like to keep Zach close to his grandparents."

"I understand." John jotted down some notes on a small pad of paper he'd pulled from his jacket pocket. "I'll have Reverend Pritchard announce your departure to the congregation next week. They'll probably want to throw you a farewell reception."

"That's fine. Zach's camp will be finished in a few weeks."

The bishop put his notebook away and rose. "I'll be praying for you, Nathan—that God finds the right placement for you. And that you'll achieve the peace of mind you're seeking."

"Thank you, John. I appreciate everything you're doing. I'm only sorry I let you down."

John frowned. "You didn't let me down. You're doing what's best for you and your son after an unspeakable tragedy. I respect you for that."

Nathan's chest constricted. "Thank you. That means a lot."

When the door closed behind John, Nathan sank back into his chair and let the air whoosh out of him. He would miss this parish family. They were a wonderful group of people. It was just unfortunate the way things had worked out.

On the bright side, he was getting a chance for a fresh start with people who didn't know his tragic history. He and Zach would start over and make a good life together, wherever God chose to use him.

After he locked up the office, Nathan stepped out into

the fresh air and sunlight, feeling some of his burden had been lifted. It was such a beautiful day, he decided to walk the two blocks to the rectory—the last step in facing his past. He needed to return to his home, no matter how many painful memories it held.

The small two-bedroom bungalow had changed very little since he left, except for the long fringes of grass that partly obscured the walkway to the front door. Nathan couldn't help but remember coming here for the first time with Cynthia as a newlywed and how excited they'd been to move into their first house.

The door stuck as he turned the key, and he used his hip to push it open. Immediately, a wall of hot air hit him. He made his way in, grimacing at the stale, musty smell. He strode into the kitchen, where he pulled open the window over the sink to let the air in. He did the same in the living and dining room, before he took a moment to be still and look around.

Everything appeared exactly as he had left it. The over-stuffed brown couch and love seat, the faded area rug with a few of Zach's remote-controlled cars and action figures still scattered about. He remembered the panicked state he'd been in when he'd left, suffocating in anxiety, desperately needing a change of scenery.

His glance fell on the small pile of cardboard boxes in the corner of the room by the door. *The last of Cynthia's things*. Right after the funeral, her parents had cleared all her belongings out of the apartment where she and Zach had been living and had everything sent over to the rectory.

Nathan walked down the hall to Zach's room and smiled at the customary mess. Despite the clutter, there wouldn't be a lot to pack up when they moved. One toy box and a closet of clothes, maybe a few more things in the garage.

He closed the door and moved down the hall to the room he had shared with Cynthia. His steps slowed and he hesitated before turning the knob. Nothing but silence greeted him when he opened the door. What had he expected? Cynthia's ghost to jump out and berate him?

The room was as barren as he had left it. He'd gotten rid of nearly everything after Cynthia's betrayal. Yet while the physical reminders of his wife may be gone, the specter of memories, mostly bad ones, remained. He closed his eyes and waited for the pain and guilt to kick in, but only a slight sadness washed over him. He rolled his shoulders to dispel the tension and felt himself begin to relax. Slowly, he opened his eyes and looked around the room, trying to be objective.

If he were honest, it was an ugly space—devoid of personality or style. That had been one of Cynthia's main complaints after they'd lived there a while. And Nathan knew now she had been right. Why hadn't he listened to her at the time?

"I'm sorry, Cynthia," he said aloud, "for not being a better husband, for not respecting your needs. I forgive you for leaving me. I hope you can forgive me, too."

His words hung in the air. Though he had no tangible proof of forgiveness, a sense of peace invaded his heart.

On a sudden burst of energy, he strode out to the garage, grabbed a few empty cardboard boxes and brought them inside. Over the course of the next two hours, he filled six cartons with books, photos and other personal items that he wouldn't need in the near future. He piled the boxes in the living room with the others, then grabbed a bottle of water from the fridge.

As he prepared to leave the house, he became more convinced than ever that he'd made the right decision. He and Zach would make a fresh start in a new town, in a new house. He would let Zach decorate his room however he wanted. Their next house would be a true home for his son. He would make sure of it.

Nathan remembered to close the windows before he turned out the lights and stood in the entrance, taking one last look at his former home. Then, with a turn of the key, Nathan closed the door to that chapter of his life and walked away.

Chapter Sixteen

"So what's the deal with you and Porter?" From the driver's seat of his Mustang, Matt speared Paige with a questioning glance.

Once they were certain their father would make a full recovery, Matt had insisted on driving her back to Wyndermere, and since she'd already told Nathan not to wait for her, she'd had no excuse to refuse her brother's offer.

Paige kept her eyes glued to the road ahead and struggled not to groan. This was the main reason she'd wanted to take a bus back. "I told you. I'm counseling his son."

"And?"

"And we've become friends."

He snorted. "Friends? I saw the way the guy was looking at you."

Her irritation rose. "You're seeing things that aren't there."

"Yeah, well, call me crazy, but I'd say the guy's in love with you."

Her heart stopped in her chest for a good ten seconds before it thumped to life again. "No," she whispered. "You're wrong."

"I don't think so." He raised an eyebrow. "And judging from your reaction, I'd say you're halfway gone yourself."

Warmth flooded her cheeks as she glared at him. "You are so off base it's not funny."

He only snorted again.

What was it about brothers that made you want to kill them? She clamped her mouth shut and stared out the window, unsettled by her own thoughts. Could Matt be right about Nathan? Was he in love with her?

With all her heart, she prayed he was wrong. Paige did not want to be responsible for any more heartache for Nathan. Because no matter what she felt or didn't feel, there could be no future for them.

Almost losing her father had only reinforced her decision not to risk loving again. Waiting to hear whether her dad would live or die, she'd relived the same terror as when she'd lost Colin. God was sending her a message—one she received loud and clear.

About an hour outside Pine Ridge, Matt stopped to gas up and grab some burgers at a roadside restaurant. Matt wiped his chin with his sleeve, caught her watching and grinned sheepishly.

She laughed. "Just like old times, except Mom's not here to yell at you." Sobering, she handed Matt a napkin. "We had a great childhood, didn't we?"

"The best."

She shuddered. "I don't know what I would have done if we'd lost Dad. I couldn't go through that type of grief again."

Matt crushed his wrapper into a ball before responding. "I know it's scary, Paige, but death is unavoidable."

She bit down on her bottom lip. "Which is why I'm never getting married."

"You can't be serious."

"I'm very serious. Losing Colin almost killed me. I can't go through anything like that again."

He shook his head. "That's a lonely way to go through life, sis. Do you really think you'll be satisfied that way? Without someone special to share your life?" He shot her another stern look. "And what about your patients? Will you build a wall around yourself to keep their grief from touching you?"

Paige's thoughts flew to Zach. Was that why she hadn't pushed him to open up more, because deep down she couldn't deal with Zach's greatest pain?

She stuck out her chin. "Remaining detached is a necessity when dealing with such intense emotions every day. I'll be a better counselor by being objective."

Matt chewed a fry. "Was Mr. Dickenson aloof and objective when he treated you? Or did you feel a real sense of caring from him?"

Paige's throat constricted as memories of Mr. Dickenson's warmth and kindness came back to her. His empathy and the knowledge that he had truly cared about her had been a big factor in helping her heal.

Matt leaned over and laid a warm hand on her arm. "You're a warm, loving, compassionate person, Paige. Don't lock half of yourself away. Your family, your friends and your future patients deserve all of you."

She let out a ragged sigh. "I'm doing the best I can, Matti." Grabbing her trash, she pushed up from her seat. "Come on. We'd better get back on the road."

He scowled but remained silent as they headed back to the car. Which was good, because she had no energy left for another argument.

The sign for Wyndermere appeared about an hour after they got back on the road. Against her will, Paige's pulse sped up at the prospect of seeing Nathan again, but she immediately squashed any lingering expectations.

Still, she had to work hard at containing her emotions while Matt parked the car outside Wyndermere's main entrance. She scanned the lobby as she entered, leaving Matt to make arrangements for a room. A few guests straggled through the hall on their way back from the dining room, but there was no sign of Nathan. Was she disappointed or relieved?

When she reached George's office, she took a deep breath and knocked.

"Come in," George called.

The sound of his voice, so solid and familiar, had her sighing in relief as she breezed through the door. "Hey, George. I'm finally back—"

The words died on her lips when she spotted Nathan across the room. He rose from the guest chair as she entered.

A flush crept up George's neck. "Paige, you're back. You didn't tell me you were coming today." He looked almost guilty. Had they been talking about her?

"Well, here I am." She avoided Nathan's eyes as George hugged her, but Nathan crossed the room to stand beside her.

"How is your father?" The sun beamed through the window to surround his head in a golden glow.

"Much better, thanks. The doctor says he should make a full recovery."

"That's good news."

"Yes, it is." She tried not to stare and focused on George instead. "I thought I'd better check in with you. I'll be back to work first thing tomorrow."

"Good. We've missed you around here." He rocked back on his heels.

The tension in the room fairly crackled around Paige.

"Matt's here," she said a little too brightly. "He wants to say hello if you have a minute."

A relieved grin broke out on George's face. "Are you kidding? Of course I do."

He strode out the door before Paige could say another word, leaving her alone with Nathan. She shifted from one foot to the other, trying to ignore how good he looked and the intense way he watched her.

She moved around a chair to keep a distance between them. "How's Zach?"

"Glad to be back. He really missed camp." Nathan leaned a hip against George's desk.

She smiled. "Good to know."

"He missed you, too." His voice was husky.

She fiddled with her purse strap on her shoulder. "How was your trip home?"

"It was…healing." He paused, then looked her in the eye. "I quit my job."

"You what?" She grasped the back of the chair to steady herself, sure she couldn't have heard him right.

"I met with the bishop, and I resigned."

Why did those few words rock her to the core? "So what are you going to do now?"

He shrugged. "The bishop has put in for a transfer. Guess I'll wait and see what God has in store for me."

A transfer? What if they sent Nathan far away—to the other side of the country? Her heart lurched at the possibility, then she reminded herself that it didn't matter where he went, since she wouldn't be part of his future. "Well, I know wherever you end up, you'll do great," she said softly.

"Thank you."

The emotion in his eyes reminded her why she needed to keep her distance.

"I really have to catch up with Jerry and Sandy. I'll see you later." She stepped out the door, but he followed her into the hall.

"Paige, is everything all right?"

Steeling herself, she turned. "Everything's fine."

She thought he was going to challenge her, but he only nodded.

"You must be tired from your trip. We'll talk more to-morrow."

Paige managed a stiff smile, then continued down the corridor and pushed out the door. She needed to find her friends and get an update on what had been going on in her absence. After checking the cafeteria, she headed down to the lake.

Paige scanned the crowd but failed to see her friends among them. A couple of teenage aids were supervising the energetic group in a rousing game of beach volleyball. Paige chuckled as the ball bounced right into the water, causing whoops of amusement from the opposing team.

"Paige."

The delighted cry of a child caught her attention. She looked over to see Zach flying toward her. She laughed out loud as he fell in the sand, and pulled himself back up. The joy on his face as he threw himself at her brought tears to her eyes. She caught him up in a huge bear hug, not even minding the damp swimsuit or the scratch of sand.

"How are you?" she said as she set him down.

"Great. Want to join our team?"

"I'd love to, but I can't right now. I have to find Jerry and Sandy."

Disappointment clouded Zach's eyes.

She tousled his wind-blown curls. "I need to catch up on the work I missed, but I'll be with you all day tomorrow. You and I need to have some time to talk, too."

"Okay," he agreed, brightening. "I think Jerry's in the boathouse. See you later. I gotta go before they start losing."

She laughed as he raced back to the beach. Nothing like kids to cheer you up.

After a last glance at the volleyball game, she turned toward the boathouse. Jerry was most likely tidying up for the day. Diligent as ever.

The boards on the dock made no sound as she approached the small enclosure. She opened the door, squinting into the dim interior. She was about to call out when the sight before her robbed her of speech. Jerry and Sandy stood locked together in a passionate embrace, oblivious to everything else around them.

A series of startling emotions washed over Paige as she stared at the pair, beginning with astonishment and ending in unbridled anger.

"Is this how you do your job when I'm not here?" The furious words erupted from her mouth before rational thought could overtake her.

The startled pair flew apart and stood gaping at her. Jerry was the first to recover. "Paige, you're back."

"Please, don't let me interrupt. I'm sure the teenagers are more than happy to cover for you."

Ignoring Sandy's beet-red face, Paige wheeled out the door and tore back down the dock, feet pounding on the wooden boards. She kept running, her breath coming in great gasps, finally forcing her to stop for air. She bent over her knees, chest heaving, until she could breathe normally again.

Erratic thoughts zigzagged through her brain. When she'd first discovered signs of a budding romance between Jerry and Sandy, she'd been happy for them. So why was this kiss giving her an anxiety attack?

She continued walking until she came to a clearing that led down to the lake. Paige sank onto a wooden bench and stared at the ripples that hugged the shore. The image of Jerry's hands caressing Sandy's back played over and over in her mind—a haunting reminder of what she'd never have again if she kept to her resolution to avoid relationships. Her stomach did a somersault at the painful realization that her anger stemmed from jealousy.

She envied Jerry and Sandy's relationship.

As much as she wished she could deny it, she craved

that type of connection with Nathan—longed to feel his touch, the thrill of his kiss.

A cold splash of reality jarred her hard. Despite every effort to the contrary, she was falling in love with Nathan!

She jumped to her feet and practically sprinted down the path toward the inn, consumed by the overwhelming need to get away. To go somewhere quiet where she could think.

The parking lot came into view. Matt's car was there. He wouldn't mind if she borrowed it for a while. She pulled out her key ring, which thankfully had a spare for the car, and hopped into the driver's seat. She left Matt a brief voice mail, then started up the engine. As she turned onto the main road, and the inn grew smaller in the background of her rearview mirror, relief spilled through her tense frame. Slowly, her frenzied heart rate returned to normal.

Before she knew it, she had turned down the road to the church, somehow realizing that prayer was the only thing that could help her sort out her mixed emotions.

The church's interior sat in darkness except for one small light above the altar and two on the side walls. She slid into a pew, wanting to pray, but no words would come. She absorbed the silence for a while until her thoughts calmed.

Lord, I don't understand why You brought Nathan into my life. Is it to test my faith? To prove I was serious about the path I've chosen for my life?

She became aware of the tears falling when she felt the wetness on her folded hands.

I don't want to love again, Lord. It's too hard, too scary. Please take away these feelings. Let me feel peace again.

"Paige?" The quiet voice broke the stillness, startling Paige from her thoughts.

She looked up to see Dan Redding standing in the aisle, concern in his warm eyes. Embarrassed, she swiped at her cheeks. "Dan. I thought you'd be home by now."

"I'm heading there now, but I thought I heard someone out here. Is everything okay? Your father's recovering, isn't he?"

"Dad's doing much better. I'm just worried about a personal problem. I'll be fine."

He reached out to cover her hand with his. "Can I help?"

Her lip trembled anew. "I appreciate the offer, but no."

"Does this have anything to do with Nathan?"

Paige's head flew up. "Why would you say that?"

Dan's lips lifted and he sat down beside her. "I've seen the two of you together. Saw how you reacted during the storm. If I'm not mistaken, there are a lot of feelings there on both sides."

More tears leaked down her cheeks. "I can't do this, Dan. I can't take a chance like that again."

Dan put a comforting arm around her shoulder. "It's only natural to be scared after losing someone you loved. But maybe it's time to stop fighting so hard to control everything. Why not turn things over to God? Let Him take the lead."

She only shook her head, words failing her.

"Trust God, Paige. Trust His plan for you. He won't let you down." He gave her arm a sympathetic pat as he rose. "Feel free to stay as long as you need. I'll come back and lock up later."

She sagged farther into the pew until her spine hit the hard wooden back. Was Dan right? Did she really lack trust in God's plan for her life? If so, how did she learn to unclench the death grip on her emotions and give up the rigid control she'd fought so hard to achieve?

Lord, help me to put my trust in You.

Paige stayed awhile longer, reluctant to leave the sanctuary the church provided. A gradual calmness crept over her as she sat in the dark—feeling God's presence there with her. Somehow she knew He would show her the right path to take.

Long after the sun had gone down, she returned to the car, hoping that when the time came, she could accept God's will—whatever that turned out to be.

Chapter Seventeen

The next morning, after seeing Matt off, Paige walked with Zach beside the lake. The day had dawned clear with no morning mist, and Paige had taken it as a good omen for the day ahead. She'd started out with an apology to Jerry and Sandy for her outburst the previous day. Both were gracious enough to accept her sketchy explanation of being stressed and overtired.

She turned her focus to Zach. They were running low on time and she still needed to uncover the memories of his most painful experience—finding his mother's body. She hoped he was ready to face it.

"I'd like to talk to you about the day your mother died," Paige said in a quiet voice after they'd walked for several minutes.

Zach picked up a stone to skip over the water. "I don't wanna talk about that."

"I know it's hard. After this, you'll never have to talk about it with me again if you don't want to."

When he only shrugged, she led him to a flat rock that jutted over the water. "This is my favorite spot. Let's sit here."

Without a word, he followed her up to the craggy area. She had never pushed him during any of their sessions, but she would today. She hoped the consequences wouldn't be too severe.

"Zach, I want you to tell me what happened that day, starting from the beginning."

He picked up a stick and began to poke it into the rock, swirling the gravel into the cracks, but remained silent.

"It was a school day, wasn't it?" she prompted.

He nodded.

"Did your mother wake you up?"

After several seconds, he shook his head. "We slept in and we were late. We didn't have time for breakfast."

"That must've upset her."

"It did. Mom hated being late."

Paige waited patiently for him to continue when he was ready.

"She walked me to school like she always did and we made it just in time. She was happy about that."

"What did your mother do while you were at school?"

"I don't know. Laundry, cleaning and stuff, I guess."

He unearthed a flat stone, which he promptly flung out into the water. "She told me to come straight home after school because we had to go shopping for new shoes." He wrinkled his nose. "I hate getting new shoes. They always hurt at first."

She smiled at him. "Yeah, they do. So you came right home. What happened then?"

Zach looked away.

Interesting body language. He was hiding something.

"When I got home, she was lying on the couch. I thought she was asleep, but when I called she wouldn't wake up. I...I went to shake her. She was really cold and wouldn't open her eyes." He dragged a grimy hand over his face, leaving a trail of dirt in its wake. "I got scared and called my grandma. She told me she would be right there and she called the ambulance."

Sympathy welled at the idea of a small boy alone and terrified. "Did you wait inside the house?"

He hung his head, scraping his fingers along the cracks in the rock. "No. I went out on the front steps."

She lowered her voice, trying to be gentle. "Do you think you knew she was dead?"

He shrugged and scraped harder, blood beginning to ooze from his fingers. "I knew something was wrong. I was too scared to stay inside."

"Who arrived first?"

"They got there pretty much at the same time. My grandma stayed with me and the men went inside to help my mom. Only it was too late." His voice cracked. He looked down at his bleeding fingers, then jumped up and started to descend the craggy rocks.

Paige followed. She wasn't going to let him get away at this crucial point. "Zach, you know this wasn't your fault. Something went wrong inside your mom's brain. There was nothing anybody could do to save her."

He kept walking without looking at her. When she caught up with him, she reached out a hand to stop him. Tears had streaked through the dirt on his cheeks.

"I know it's hard to talk about this," she said. "But I need to make sure you're not feeling guilty about something you shouldn't."

When he looked up at her, anger glinted through his tears. "You can't fix everything."

He jerked free from her grasp and took off running. Her first instinct was to go after him, but after two steps, she stopped. He needed time alone to process his emotions. Zach was feeling some measure of guilt over his mother's death, and she'd have to work hard over the next week to make sure he dealt with it before camp ended.

Because if he didn't, the results could be disastrous.

Nathan pulled a five iron from his bag and hit the ball straight down the fairway onto the green.

"Nice shot." Dan whistled, then picked up his clubs.

"More like lucky shot." Nathan grinned.

The two headed to the green.

"You seem much more relaxed today," Dan observed. "Quitting your job must agree with you."

Nathan chuckled. "Seems so. I must say it's a relief to have made a decision. Now all I have to do is enjoy my time off until the bishop calls with a new placement."

Dan gave him a strange look. "That brings me to the topic I wanted to talk to you about."

Nathan set down his clubs on the edge of the green, not sure what to expect.

"I received word yesterday that I've been approved to hire an assistant pastor at the church. With the size of the parish increasing so rapidly, I can't do everything myself anymore. My family is seeing less and less of me. You know how stressful that can be."

"All too well. An assistant will be a big help."

Dan took out his putter and leaned on it. "The fact is, Nathan, you're the man I'd like to see join our team. You have all the qualities I need in an assistant pastor, and I know you'd fit in well here."

Nathan blinked. "You're offering me a job?"

"That's right. I haven't got all the particulars yet as to salary and benefits, but I wanted to give you first crack at it. And time to think about whether you'd be interested in moving out this way."

"Wow. I'm flattered at the offer, Dan."

"I sense a *but* coming."

Nathan raked his hand through his hair. "Not necessarily. This has come out of the blue though. I'll need some time to think it over. And talk to Zach."

"Of course. In the meantime, I'll try to get more details about the position."

Nathan smiled and held out his hand. "Thanks for the vote of confidence. I appreciate it."

Dan shook his hand warmly. "I hope you take the job. I have a feeling we'd make an unbeatable team."

After finishing the game, Nathan took the long route back to Wyndermere, giving him time to think about Dan's offer. As assistant pastor, Nathan wouldn't be under as much pressure as he had been back at Saint Stephen's. He could ease his way back to work. He already liked the people in the community, and since they weren't tainted by the stain of Nathan's past, he could start over with a clean slate.

The area was a good one for raising kids. Zach would flourish here, Nathan was sure. They would be near George and Catherine for support. The one drawback would be taking Zach away from both sets of grandparents.

The MacNeals. His stomach twisted as he imagined their reaction. They hadn't been happy that Zach was going away to camp for the whole summer, never mind moving here permanently. Would his decision only antagonize Charlotte further? Make her even more determined to get custody?

Nathan forced himself to breathe normally and not let himself be consumed by fear. He couldn't base his and Zach's future on his mother-in-law's bullying tactics. Besides, if the MacNeals did take him to court, Nathan now felt equipped to handle the fight. His relationship with Zach was stronger than ever. Zach's emotional state had improved considerably, and with Paige's professional testimony, Nathan felt confident they could counteract any claim to the contrary. The last area of concern, Nathan's unemployment, would also become a nonissue if Nathan accepted Dan's job. Nathan doubted any judge would remove Zach from his custody under these new circumstances.

The last band of tension loosened from Nathan's chest. The more he considered the idea of working with Dan, the more excited he got. This job—this move—might be the very thing they needed to put the tragedy behind them, once and for all.

His thoughts turned to Paige, and his excitement waned. Nathan still hadn't given up hope of a future relationship, once they were both sure they were ready. At least in the city, he would've been close to the college she attended. Out here, he'd be hours away. He wouldn't see her for months at a time. But could he base a decision this big on Paige's education schedule? No, if God meant for them to be together, He would see that things worked out. In His perfect timing.

Alone in his room, Nathan prayed and contemplated the offer. The more he considered it from every angle, the more convinced he became that God was leading him to take the position. However, he had one more hurdle to overcome.

Zach had to want this, too. Nathan wouldn't risk damaging the fragile relationship they'd forged by forcing him to do something he hated the thought of. Nathan prayed God would help him convince Zach when he got a chance to talk to him alone.

It was almost supper time before Nathan managed to catch up with Zach, at the end of horseback riding lessons. Nathan stood at the fence by the pasture and watched Zach atop the large horse, so confident and relaxed, laughing with his friend Peter. It was amazing how far Zach had come. When the boys had dismounted, Zach spotted him and came racing over.

"Did you see me, Dad? I was riding Horatio." The boy's face beamed excitement.

"Doing a fine job, too." Nathan smiled at Zach's enthusiasm. "If you're done, do you think you could spare a few minutes for your dad?"

As though sensing the serious nature of the talk, Zach sobered. "Sure, I guess. Just let me tell them."

A few seconds later, he returned. "It's okay. Jerry and Peter will groom my horse for me."

"Great. Let's go for a walk."

Zach frowned. "Is something wrong, Dad?"

"No. In fact, I have some good news. At least I hope you'll think so." They turned off onto the path by the water. Somehow it was hard to get the words out. "I've been offered a job at the church, working with Reverend Dan."

"Oh."

Nathan waited for more of a reaction and when none came, he continued. "We could get a little house around here. I'll find out where the nearest school is. And we'd be close to George and Catherine. You could even come over and visit the horses and the kittens."

That brought a gleam to Zach's eyes. "I could?"

"Sure. And maybe we could even get that dog you've always wanted." Nathan cringed at openly bribing his son to love the idea.

"Really? My own dog?"

"Yeah. But you'd have to promise to walk him every day."

"I will. No problem."

They walked in silence for a while as Zach contemplated this new development. Nathan hoped his silence meant he accepted the idea.

"What about Paige?" Zach asked out of the blue a few minutes later.

"What about her?"

"Will she still live here at Wyndermere?"

Nathan couldn't quite meet his gaze. "No, Zach. She's going back to school in the fall."

"I won't see her anymore after camp is over?"

Nathan saw the distress on his son's face and knew exactly how he felt. But he put on a brave front. "Maybe at Thanksgiving or Christmas when we go to the city for a visit."

"Oh." The light slid out of his eyes.

"You can email her. And phone her."

"It won't be the same."

Nathan's heart cracked a little for his son. Zach's dependence on Paige was worse than Nathan had imagined. He'd have to speak to her about it and ask her to begin the disengaging process. "No, it won't. It'll take some time to adjust...no matter where we end up living."

Zach scuffed the toe of his sneaker on the path. "I guess if I had to choose, I'd pick here. I really like it here, Dad." His face brightened. "If we have our own house, maybe we could adopt Willy, too."

A cat and a dog? Nathan swallowed, remembering his vow to make their next house a real home for his son. A couple of pets seemed a reasonable price to pay. "I think we could find room for Willy."

Zach whooped and reached over to hug Nathan around the waist. "Thanks, Dad."

Nathan ruffled Zach's hair. "You're welcome."

While he walked Zach back to join the other campers, his thoughts turned once again to Paige. He needed to have a serious conversation with her very soon. The summer was almost over, and if he didn't try one more time to start a relationship with her, he'd regret it the rest of his life. He didn't fool himself into thinking her reaction would be completely positive, but Nathan wasn't ready to let their chance at happiness end without a fight.

Chapter Eighteen

Paige threw her full weight into the shovel as she flung the clean straw into Mabel's stall. The physical effort helped relieve the frustration and inner tension that percolated under her skin. Her unwanted feelings for Nathan continued to plague her, compounding her exasperation over not pinning Zach down to more counseling time. After his outburst at the lake, he'd avoided her, as though afraid she might pry the truth out of him. She couldn't shake the feeling that he was hiding something about the day his mother died. If so, she needed to help him deal with it once and for all.

She blew the hair off her forehead and stepped out of the stall, only to jump back in alarm at the sight of a man standing in the aisle. Visions of Brandon Marshall swirled through her brain, and it took a moment to realize it was Nathan. Her nerves skipped into overdrive for a different reason.

"Sorry. Didn't mean to startle you." He took a step toward her.

"It's okay." She closed the stall door and latched the bolt.

"Could I speak to you for a minute?" An aura of unease swirled around him.

Self-consciously, she tried to smooth her hair back into the elastic and brush the straw from her jeans. Nathan was perfectly groomed as usual in a polo shirt and neatly pressed khaki pants. "As long as you don't mind following me. I've got some chores to finish before the campfire."

"Lead the way."

She headed through the barn to the shelf that held the water pails and turned on the hose.

"What can I do for you?" She began to fill the containers without looking at him, figuring he wanted an update on Zach's progress.

"I wanted to tell you my news."

She straightened and turned off the water. "What news?" The muscles across her shoulders tightened.

He leaned against the wall, arms crossed. "Dan Redding offered me a job as assistant pastor at his church."

Paige's mouth fell open. "You're kidding."

He grinned. "That's how I felt when he first told me. But after thinking about it, I feel it could be the right move for Zach and me."

She blinked, trying to absorb the idea of Nathan working at the Pine Ridge church. His face radiated hope, free at last from the guilt and sorrow that had weighed on him so heavily when they first met. "You seem pleased with the idea."

"I am." He bent to pick up one of the pails. "All summer I've been thinking how much I love it here. The fresh air, open spaces, the friendly people. Now I don't have to leave it all behind."

"How did Zach take the news?"

"Overall, I'd say he's excited. Of course, the promise of a dog sweetened the pot."

Her lips twitched. "That would help."

"It will be a fresh start for both of us. Away from all the bad memories."

She picked up a bucket and headed toward Horatio's stall. "I'm glad for you, Nathan. I know Zach will love it here, once he settles in and makes some friends."

They set down the pails near the stall door and Nathan

took her gently by the shoulders. She attempted to quell the flutters in the pit of her stomach.

"Everything is almost perfect," he said.

The way he looked at her made her tingle inside. Instinctively she knew she didn't want to hear what was coming next, but found herself powerless to stop him. When he reached down to take her hand in his, she didn't even try to move.

"Paige, it's no secret that I've come to develop strong feelings for you. You've changed my life for the better in so many ways. I'm not ready to let you out of my life."

Her heart battled to escape her chest. Part of her rejoiced at hearing his feelings for her. The larger part, however, quaked in terror.

"I know you're going back to school," he continued, "and I have no intention of interfering with that." His fingers squeezed hers. "I'm asking you to keep an open mind about the possibility of a future together. I'll wait as long as it takes—until you're ready."

She held up a hand. "Stop, please. You don't understand." It was hard to take air into her lungs with sheer panic suffocating her.

He stepped closer, confusion swimming in his eyes. "Then help me understand."

His nearness overwhelmed her. One kiss and she'd be lost. Her nerves, already on edge, shredded to the breaking point. "I'm sorry. I can't do this. It's too hard."

His features darkened. He let go of her, but didn't step away. "If you can look me in the eye and tell me you don't have feelings for me, I'll never bother you again."

Anguish threatened to buckle her knees. How she wished she could lie and tell him she felt nothing. She shook her head. "Please, just forget about me, Nathan. It's the best—for everyone."

She backed away, inadvertently upsetting one of the pails

in the process. A flood of water spilled over her feet onto the floor, but she ignored it. With a sob, she ran from the barn, leaving the soggy mess behind.

Back in the cabin, Paige yanked off her waterlogged shoes and threw them at the wall in disgust. She'd done it this time. She'd finally severed ties with Nathan for good. She pulled on clean socks and laced up her spare sneakers. Remorse consumed her, recalling the hurt that had filled Nathan's face. All he'd ever done was offer her his strength and affection, and she'd treated him terribly in return.

She swiped impatient fingers across her cheeks to dash away the tears that kept falling. She had no right to cry. She'd brought this all on herself by letting her guard down, and allowing Nathan to get too close. It made her want something she didn't have the courage to claim.

Paige pushed up from the bed and focused on getting ready for the sing-along. She took a deep breath to pull herself together and headed outside, praying that Nathan would be nowhere near the campfire tonight.

Nathan knocked on the Reddings' front door and shoved his fisted hands into his pockets.

"Nathan? This is a surprise." Gwen smiled in welcome. "Please come in."

"Thanks. Sorry to drop by unannounced."

"Don't be silly. You don't need a formal invitation." She gestured for him to follow her down the hall. "Dan's in the study. Can I bring you a cup of coffee?"

He tried to will his bad mood away and managed a weak smile. "No, thanks."

Gwen paused to peer up at him. "Are you okay?"

He shrugged. "Not having my best day."

"I'm sorry. I know what that's like." She gestured to the open doorway. "Go on in."

Dan looked up in surprise as Nathan knocked on the open door.

"Nathan. What brings you by?"

Something about the man's easy nature made the coil of tension inside him begin to unwind. Nathan moved farther into the room. "I wanted to tell you in person that I've decided to accept your job offer."

A smile broke out on Dan's face. "Well, that is good news." He rose and held out his hand. "I'm very pleased to have you on board."

Nathan shook his hand and took a seat across from the man who would be his boss.

"I'm assuming Zach agreed or you wouldn't be doing this."

"With a bribe. I promised him a new dog."

Dan chuckled and shook his head. "You may be sorry about that."

Nathan shrugged. "Could be worse. Could be a horse."

Dan laughed again, then got serious. "I get the feeling something else is on your mind tonight."

Nathan slumped in the chair as if the air had leaked out of him. "That obvious?"

"Let's just say I'd hoped for a bit more enthusiasm."

"Sorry. It's not the job, believe me." Nathan rose to pace the small room. Could he dump his problems on Dan? What would be the point anyway? No one could fix the situation. And yet he felt as if he might explode if he couldn't talk this out with someone.

"Is it Paige?" Dan's voice was gentle, encouraging.

Nathan nodded. "I finally got the nerve to tell her I had feelings for her and that I was willing to wait until she was ready for a relationship."

"That sounds reasonable."

Nathan gave a wry laugh. "I thought so, too. But she

got upset and bolted out the door so fast…" His throat constricted, too dry to continue.

Dan came around to lean a hip against the desk. "What did she say?"

"She told me to forget about her. Can't get much clearer than that."

Dan crossed his arms, frowning. "That doesn't sound like her."

Nathan blew out a long breath. "I guess I have to face the facts. Paige is not interested in a relationship with me. Simple as that." A mantle of sadness weighed down his shoulders at the thought.

The floorboards creaked in the hall. Gwen appeared in the doorway, a sheepish expression on her face. She entered the room carrying a mug. "I wasn't eavesdropping. I came to bring Nathan some herbal tea. It helps ease tension." She handed him the cup, not quite meeting his eyes.

"Thank you, Gwen." He took a quick sip of the tea and smothered a grimace at the bitter taste.

Gwen hovered beside the desk. "I'm so sorry about Paige, Nathan. But I think you're wrong about her feelings."

He straightened and set the cup down. "What do you mean?"

She bit her bottom lip. "I don't want to betray a confidence, but I can't stand by and watch her throw away this chance at happiness for you both."

A flutter of hope rose in his chest. Nathan waited while Gwen seemed to wrestle with her conscience.

She looked at Dan and back to Nathan. "You know about Colin, right?"

"Yes, she told me about the accident."

Gwen closed her eyes for a moment and when she opened them, a determined light shone in their depths. "After Colin died, Paige made a promise to herself." Gwen sighed. "A promise never to marry. To devote her life to helping her patients."

Nathan sank onto one of the chairs, processing her words. "That was four years ago. Don't you think it's possible she'll change her mind?"

Gwen shrugged. "I don't know. She's terrified of losing someone she loves again. She's never allowed anyone to get close. But you and Zach got through her barriers. I may be wrong, but I think she has real feelings for you." She reached out to lay a hand on his arm. "Don't give up too easily, Nathan. You'll never find a more honest, caring person than Paige. She's worth the effort, I promise."

Paige tried to get into the spirit of the sing-along, but her heart wasn't in it. Trying to push her feelings aside, she concentrated on a rousing rendition of "The Bear Went Over the Mountain." When they finished the song, a nagging sense of disquiet snaked up her spine. Something wasn't right, but she couldn't put her finger on it.

She scanned the group before her, and when she spied Peter and Kyle sitting together, it hit her like the pail of cold water she'd spilled in the barn.

Zach wasn't there!

Sweat broke out on Paige's forehead. How could she not have noticed? Rising from the bench, she clapped her hands for attention. "Has anyone seen Zach?"

A murmur rippled through the kids. Beside her, Jerry and Sandy rose also. Paige moved toward Peter, who sat with his gaze glued to the ground. "Peter, do you know where Zach went?"

The boy looked up, his eyes awash with misery. "Is Zach in trouble?"

Paige knelt beside the child. "No, but you need to tell me the truth."

The boy hesitated, then released a breath. "He went to see his kitten."

"When?"

"Right after dinner."

"Are you sure?"

When the boy nodded, Paige's stomach clenched. That meant Zach had been in the barn at the same time she and Nathan were talking. He must have overheard their whole conversation.

Paige rose slowly. "Thanks, honey. You've been a big help." She turned to Jerry. "Can I speak to you for a minute?"

They left Sandy in charge and headed over to the barn on the off chance that Zach might still be there.

"Nathan and I had an argument earlier," she told Jerry as they walked. "I think Zach may have overheard us."

Jerry frowned. "What were you arguing about?"

Paige picked up the pace, annoyed at the heat rising to her cheeks. "It doesn't matter." They had reached the barn, and Paige paused, her hand on the latch. "The bottom line is that if Zach overheard us, he's probably pretty upset."

"What about Nathan?"

"He was upset, too."

"Could he have taken Zach and left?"

"It's possible. But my instinct says no."

Jerry's mouth set into a grim line. "I trust your instincts. Let's check here and a few other spots before we panic. No sense in worrying Porter if we find Zach first."

Twenty minutes later with no sign of Zach, Paige could feel hysteria bubbling up in waves. "It's all my fault, Jerry. If something happens to him, I'll never forgive myself."

He turned angry eyes on her. "You need to stop thinking like that and get a grip on yourself. We're going to find him, but I need you to stay calm."

She took a deep breath, counted to ten and exhaled. "Okay, what do we do next?"

Jerry turned toward the lake. "We'd better check the water. And call in more searchers."

Dread mixed with the panic rolling in her stomach. "I guess I have no choice. I'll have to call Nathan."

But how on earth was she supposed to tell him his son was missing?

Chapter Nineteen

Nathan drove back toward Wyndermere pondering Gwen's words. *Don't give up too easily, Nathan.*

He didn't want to give up, but what else could he do to change Paige's mind?

The sound of his cell phone interrupted his thoughts.

"Nathan, it's Paige."

His pulse sprinted. Had she experienced a change of heart?

"Zach isn't with you by any chance, is he?" Her voice sounded unnatural.

Something cold and unholy skittered through his system. "What do you mean? Isn't he at the campfire with you?"

Paige's hesitation told him what his gut already knew.

"I'm sorry, Nathan. I'm afraid Zach is missing. We have a search party looking for him now."

"What?" In one wild jerk of the wheel, he pulled over to the side of the road. The blood seemed to drain from his body. Just as quickly, anger surged up and spewed forth. "How could you lose my son?" The harshness of his tone jarred even him. He swiped a hand over his eyes, trying not to imagine the countless ways Zach could get hurt—in the woods, on the water…

Nothing but silence hummed on the other end of the phone.

"It looks like Zach may have overheard us in the barn," Paige said at last. "He could be hiding because he's upset—"

"I'm on my way." He disconnected the call, cutting her off midsentence.

As he turned the car back onto the road, Nathan began reciting every prayer he could remember.

Paige slid her phone into her pocket and blinked hard to push the moisture back. Any doubts she had about Nathan's feelings toward her after the scene in the barn were now clear. He despised her. Not only had she rejected him, she'd neglected her duties and now Zach was missing.

"Paige." A breathless Jerry ran up the path. "One of the canoes is gone. And we found Zach's hat down on the dock."

A sharp stab of fear sliced through her. Zach was out on the water, alone in the pitch-dark. Faced with that daunting reality, determination stiffened her spine. She would not allow anything to happen to him.

"Grab some flashlights," she ordered. "We're going out."

A chill had settled over the inky water as they pushed away from the dock. Paige wished she'd had time to grab a sweatshirt. The soggy life vest was not helping matters as the dampness seeped through her cotton T-shirt. Jerry paddled with fierce strokes while Paige shone the light ahead. Not a ripple broke the calm black surface.

"I wish we knew which direction to look in." Jerry huffed as he pulled on the paddle.

"Head over to the island," she said. "He wanted to go there once before. It's a long shot, but…"

"Worth a try."

Paige forced all negative thoughts out of her mind and focused with grim resolve on the water ahead. The farther out on the water they went, the blacker it became, with only the beam of the flashlight visible in front of them. The sound of the paddle slicing the water broke the incredible stillness surrounding them. After ten minutes of silent paddling that yielded no results, Paige's hope began to waver. She squinted out over the dark expanse. Could Zach really have traveled this far by himself?

She closed her eyes and sent silent prayers out into the night.

Lord, guide us to where he is. And please keep him safe until we find him.

Nathan screeched the car to a halt in the inn's parking lot. George stood waiting for him, arms crossed and feet braced. From the harsh set of his friend's features, Nathan knew they hadn't found his son.

"They think Zach's out on the lake," George told him without preamble. "Jerry and Paige have gone out after him."

Nathan wasn't sure which fact caused him the greater alarm. Either way, he had to get out there, too. "You still have that dinghy with the outboard?"

"Yeah. It's down at my dock."

"Let's go."

They sprinted down to the waterfront behind George and Catherine's house. Nathan paced back and forth on the dock while George readied the boat. Nathan's thoughts spun like his car tires over gravel. Why on earth would Zach take a canoe out on the lake in the dark by himself? Nothing made sense right now.

The boat engine roared to life.

"Grab the rope," George yelled.

Nathan untied the mooring and leaped into the boat as George guided it away from the pier.

"We'll head toward the middle of the lake."

Nathan nodded, focusing the high-powered flashlight

ahead of them. For the hundredth time that night, he sent up desperate prayers to keep Zach, and now Paige, safe.

Fighting the panic that clawed at his chest, Nathan swept the surface of the water with the beam while the boat sped into the night. If anything happened to Zach, he knew he would never recover.

At last, a pinprick of light came into view, bobbing several hundred yards in the distance. He swung the flashlight toward it and made out a male figure in a canoe looking over the side into the water. The man looked up and began to wave his arms over his head. As they sped closer, Nathan recognized Jerry. An icy chill that had nothing to do with the evening air swept over him.

Where was Paige?

George cut the engine and the boat slid up beside Jerry's craft.

"She spotted Zach's overturned canoe and jumped in before I could stop her." The younger man's frantic voice matched his facial expression. Water dripped from his hair and clothing. "I went in after her, but I couldn't find them."

"How long ago?" Nathan ripped off his shoes and tossed his cell phone on the floor of the boat.

Jerry shook his head. "A minute, maybe two? I'm not sure."

"Nate! Over there." George aimed the beam of light at the water where a flurry of air bubbles broke the surface a few hundred feet away.

Immediately Nathan dived into the abyss. After a few powerful strokes, a head broke through the surface of the water. Paige sputtered and coughed, fighting to drag a dark shape up beside her. Nathan moved faster, and as he reached them, grabbed the lifeless form from her.

Zach! Fear lodged in his heart like a shard of glass, but he pushed it back. He couldn't afford to waste time on emotion. Straining every muscle in his upper torso, Nathan towed Zach to the boat.

"Take him," he gasped at George. "I'm going back for Paige."

Without a word, George pulled Zach into the dinghy.

Nathan forced the image of his son's limp body from his mind, trusting George to handle it, and turned back. After only a few strokes, he saw Paige swimming toward him. He could tell by her flailing arms that she was struggling. He swam up to her and grabbed her around the waist. Her arms came around his neck and they bobbed on the surface until she'd caught her breath.

"Hold on to my waist. I'll tow you in."

She only nodded and moved her arms to his waist. He took one long breath, and using all his strength, began to swim back.

Minutes later, when he finally reached the side of George's boat, Nathan's muscles felt weighted with lead. Strong arms reached down to pull Paige from him. Nathan choked on a mouthful of water and sputtered as he pulled himself up, thankful when George helped haul him onto the deck. Nathan caught a brief flash of two motionless figures on the floor and could only pray the people he loved most would be okay.

Chapter Twenty

"We've done all we can for your son, Mr. Porter. Now we'll have to wait and see." The doctor on call flipped the sheet back on his clipboard. "It's amazing you found him in the dark water."

The man's words provided little comfort to Nathan with Zach lying in the ICU hooked up to tubes and monitors. He dragged his gaze away from the still form of his son and shifted his attention to the gray-haired doctor at the foot of the bed. "What's your best guess at a prognosis?"

The doctor peered over his bifocals. "I wish I could tell you with any degree of certainty. But everything depends on how long Zach was submerged. I'm sorry I can't be more positive."

Nathan's throat constricted. This could not be happening. He was trapped in a nightmare and couldn't wake up. "Can I sit with him now?"

"Of course."

When the doctor left, Nathan dragged a chair over to the side of the bed, grateful at least for the dry clothes Catherine had brought him. Helpless, he stared down at Zach's pale, unmoving form on the hospital bed. An impotent rage bubbled to the surface and lodged throbbing at the base of his skull. How could this be happening, just when he thought he was getting his life back on track?

He blew out a weary breath and slumped back on the

chair. Zach's face was as colorless as the white pillow-case under his head. Nathan reached out to clasp his limp hand—so small and lifeless—in his. The light of an over-head lamp shone halo-like around his brown curls. An un-natural silence filled the room, broken only by the erratic beeps of the monitors.

"Hey, Zach. It's Dad. You're going to be okay." His gruff words echoed in the sterile space.

When there was no reaction, Nathan stroked Zach's hand. An overwhelming need to keep talking pressed him, hoping his voice, or something he said, would spark a re-sponse.

"I don't know why you ran away. But I'm not mad. We can work out whatever was bothering you. You just need to get better first." He drew in a ragged breath. "I want you to be able to tell me everything you're feeling, all your prob-lems, no matter how big or small."

Zach's eyelid twitched. Nathan's heart stopped for a sec-ond, then thudded up again.

Please, Lord. Please don't take him from me now. He's all I've got left.

His hand fisted into the sheets, holding on for dear life, as though his very sanity depended on him being physi-cally anchored here in this room. He wanted to shred the linens to ribbons, rip the wires from the machines and carry Zach home.

Instead, Nathan laid his head on his son's arm and wept.

Behind the curtained area of the exam room, Paige pulled on dry clothes, courtesy of Catherine. After check-ing the oxygen levels in her blood, the doctor had given her permission to leave, with a promise to take it easy for the next day or two. Her hands still shook, partly from the chill of the cold water, partly from the shock of all that had hap-pened. She pulled a hooded sweatshirt over her still-damp hair, wishing she could stop reliving the horror of discovering the overturned canoe and no Zach. She hadn't hesitated one second before jumping into the murky water to find him. Unlike Colin's car accident, or her father's heart attack, there was something she could do, an action she could take to protect this person whom she loved.

And maybe that was why during those moments of blinding panic, one thing had become crystal clear to her.

Life was infinitely fragile. No one was guaranteed a tomorrow. Not Colin, not her father, not even a seven-year-old boy.

And no matter how hard she'd tried to harden her heart—to keep love out of her life—she couldn't stop herself from loving.

A surge of guilt rose in her chest. The painful reality was that she *had* been holding herself back when dealing with Zach. She hadn't given him her best. Zach, and all her future patients, needed better from her.

"Your family, your friends and your future patients deserve all of you." Matt's words echoed in her head. Her brother was right. Emotional detachment would not work. As a therapist, she had to care deeply about the people she served. Just as Nathan had to care about the parishioners entrusted to his ministry.

Her heart swelled again as she recalled Nathan coming to her aid in the water. Just when she'd thought she couldn't swim another stroke, he'd shown up and helped her back to the boat. He'd left Zach to come back for her. How did she ever deserve such unselfishness, such devotion?

Paige pushed back the curtain and stepped out into the open, the truth blinding her as glaringly as the bright ER lights. Whether or not she wanted to, whether or not she'd intended to, she'd fallen in love with Zach and Nathan. What she planned to do about it, she didn't know. She could either run from that truth, or reach out and accept the love that had come unexpectedly into her life. It was a choice she'd have to make very soon, but right now, she needed to make sure Zach would be okay.

Paige's head swam as she made her way down the corridor to the elevators and up to the ICU area where she'd been told Zach was being treated. She stopped for a moment outside his room to regain her equilibrium, and then peered through a small window in the door. The breath whooshed out of her lungs. A myriad of tubes and wires snaked out of Zach's pale, lifeless body. Nathan was bent over the bed like a broken man, his shoulders heaving with silent sobs.

Paige's hand flew to her mouth, tears blurring her vision. This was all her fault. If she hadn't argued with Nathan, if she'd done her job properly and finished Zach's counseling, maybe he wouldn't have felt it necessary to run away. She took a deep breath and blinked back useless tears. No matter how Nathan felt about her, he needed her. She now had the chance to offer him the same comfort and support he'd given her on more than one occasion.

She opened the door and slipped inside. Without a word, she pulled up a stool beside Nathan's chair and sat beside him. Still bent over Zach, he didn't seem to register her presence. At last, he lifted his head and looked at her, seeming puzzled to see her there.

"Paige, are you all right?" He belatedly swiped at his red-rimmed eyes.

"I'm fine. How's Zach doing?"

His features crumpled, lines creasing his brow. "We won't know until he wakes up." A muscle worked in his neck as if he were swallowing his despair.

Paige held out her hand, and without hesitation, he grasped it—like a drowning man clinging to a lifeline.

"If it's okay, I'll wait with you."

"I'd like that." His voice sounded gravelly and hoarse.

He rubbed a thumb over the back of her hand. "You saved Zach's life. You could have died yourself."

The intensity of emotion in his gaze disconcerted her. "But I didn't. You didn't let me." She squeezed his hand. "I'm so sorry, Nathan. For everything."

He watched her with a sad, slightly puzzled expression. Finally, he nodded. "I'm just glad you're here now."

They sat for what felt like hours until at last Nathan pushed his chair back from the bed. "I have to move or I'll go crazy."

"Why don't you go find a nurse or doctor to check on Zach. I'll wait here in case he wakes up."

He threw her a grateful glance. "Thanks. I'll be back soon."

The moment he left, Paige sank back onto the seat beside the bed, more tired than she realized. She picked up Zach's hand, content to watch the steady rise and fall of his little chest. She murmured heartfelt prayers of thanks to God, and tears of gratitude returned as the full realization of just how close they'd both come to death hit her.

She would never have forgiven herself if Zach had died, all because of her argument with Nathan. Wearily she laid her head on the bed beside Zach. *Lord, what am I supposed to be learning from all this? What do You want me to do?*

The memory of a Bible verse filled her head and her heart, giving her her answer. *"Love one another as I have loved you."*

The simplicity of God's message drifted into her heart. That was all Jesus had asked of mankind, to put aside their differences, their fear and hatred, and love one another. How could she not follow God's mandate?

"Though I have all faith so that I could remove mountains, but have not love, I am nothing."

One of her mother's favorite verses from Corinthians came to mind as clearly as if her mother had been reading it to her. More tears brimmed as she studied the beautiful boy in front of her. She needed to trust God's guidance and let go of her fear. *Help me to do that, Lord.*

At that moment, Zach began to fidget. His eyes fluttered open.

Paige swiped a hand over her damp cheeks. "Hi, Zach. How are you feeling?"

He blinked twice, then managed a weak smile. "Paige?"

"Yeah, it's me."

He rubbed his eyes. "Where's Dad?"

"He went to find the doctor, but he'll be back soon. How do you feel?"

He put a hand on his chest. "It hurts here. And I'm thirsty."

She got up to pour him a glass of water, and held the straw to his lips. When he finished, she placed the cup on the side table and sat back down beside him.

"Paige, are you mad at me?" Troubled eyes held her gaze.

"No, honey. I'm not mad."

"Even though I took Jerry's canoe?"

The sadness on his face tore at her heart. She shook her head. "I'm only sad you felt you had to run away—that you didn't trust me or your dad enough to tell us what was bothering you."

Zach's chin quivered, but he didn't say a word. She picked up his hand and held it tight.

"Did you hear your dad and me arguing in the barn?" she asked softly.

He nodded.

"Did you run away because of that?"

He looked down at the sheets. "I thought if I was gone, you'd say yes to my dad. And then he'd be happy again."

Her heart spasmed at his words. "Why would you think that?"

"Because I do bad things, and God punishes me. Everyone I love leaves."

Oh, Zach. She had to cover her mouth to keep from sobbing out loud. "What bad things did you do?"

Zach fidgeted with the bedsheet. He turned away to look at the wall.

"You can tell me, Zach." She squeezed his hand.

She waited. Tears gathered on Zach's long eyelashes and slowly dropped onto his cheek.

"I didn't go straight home."

Paige frowned. "When?"

He ignored her question as his words poured out. "I didn't want to get new shoes. So I went to my friend Brian's after school."

Realization began to dawn on Paige.

"It's my fault she died." He began to sob in earnest now. "I should've come home like Mom asked. Then maybe she wouldn't be dead."

The magnitude of the guilt he'd been hiding hit her hard. "Oh, honey, no. That's not true." She pulled him tight against her, fighting to control her own emotion. "It's not your fault."

His thin shoulders shook, heaving up and down as he gulped in air, tears soaking her sweatshirt. Paige stroked his head and murmured soothing words until he quieted. She handed him a tissue to wipe his face, then cupped his chin.

"This is very important," she said, looking him in the eye. "It wouldn't have mattered if you came home any earlier. Do you understand?"

Zach sniffed and shrugged his shoulders.

"Paige is right."

She looked up to see a very solemn Nathan standing in the doorway. Dark circles under his eyes stood out against the paleness of his face.

"For a long time I blamed myself for your mother dying because we had a fight. But I've talked to a few doctors and they all say the same thing. It didn't happen because she was upset or angry. It just happened. No matter what we did that day, it still would have happened, and there's nothing we could have done to stop it."

Relief spilled through Paige. It appeared Nathan had finally let go of his own guilt over Cynthia's death. Now if only Zach could do the same.

Nathan moved to the other side of the bed. "Is that why you ran away? Because you felt guilty?"

Zach looked away, misery etched in his eyes.

Paige knew Nathan had to hear the truth. "Zach thought if he went away, I would stay with you."

Nathan frowned. "I don't understand. Why did you think that?"

Zach shrugged again but looked up at his father. "I thought Paige knew how bad I was. That's why she wouldn't say yes. I thought if I went away…"

"Oh, Zach. You couldn't be more wrong." Moisture glistened in Nathan's eyes. "You are the most important person in the world to me. And as much as I care about Paige, I would never choose her over you."

Nathan pulled Zach into his arms, wires and all. The boy clung to his father like a burr, his wiry arms wrapped tight around Nathan's neck. Tears rolled down Nathan's face.

Feeling like an intruder on this intimate scene, Paige ducked out of the room to give them some privacy. Nathan needed this crucial time alone with Zach, and she needed some time to sort through her thoughts and feelings.

One thing was certain—she and Nathan would have to have a serious talk before he and Zach left Wyndermere.

Chapter Twenty-One

The final campfire sing-along had been a resounding success with a good number of adults from the inn adding their eclectic mix of voices to the performance. After the kids had settled into the cabin for their last night together, Paige left Sandy with the girls and set off in search of Nathan. Tomorrow he would be leaving. She couldn't put off this talk any longer.

Many of the adults had remained outside on the patio to enjoy the beautiful evening, seeming reluctant to have their idyllic time at Wyndermere come to an end. Paige greeted the guests as she made her way through the crowd, accepting compliments on her singing and guitar playing. It didn't surprise her not to find Nathan among the group.

Her gaze swung down toward the water, where the glow of the setting sun silhouetted a lone figure standing on the end of the dock. Paige's heart hiccupped in her chest at the sight of him, so tall and steady. What was he thinking about all alone down there?

Quietly, she made her way across the lawn, over the small stretch of sand to the wooden pier. If Nathan heard her approaching footsteps, he gave no indication, remaining still, hands in his pockets, staring out over the calm lake, where only the smallest of ripples disturbed the glass surface.

Paige came up beside him and stood looking out at the horizon. The last trace of sunset lingered over the water.

"Beautiful, isn't it?" she whispered.

"It is. I'll miss this view." The melancholy tone of his voice resonated inside her.

"So will I." Why did the words she'd been so eager to share with Nathan now seem stuck in her throat?

Before she could think of how to start, Nathan turned to face her. Her breath caught at the stark emotion shimmering in his blue eyes.

"I don't even know how to begin to thank you for everything you've done for us. You've given us our lives back. I could never have come this far without you."

"Nathan, I—"

"No, please let me finish. I've been rehearsing this speech for when we leave tomorrow, but I'd rather say it now."

Paige's heart cracked a little at the sorrow evident on his face, but she only nodded.

"I owe you an apology for my selfishness. For presuming to know how you feel, for trying to coerce you into something you're not ready for."

When Paige opened her mouth to protest, he held up a hand to stop her. "I'm not done."

A light breeze ruffled the hair over his forehead. Paige gripped her hands together to keep from reaching out to smooth it down.

"You've become an important part of Zach's life, and I hope…I hope my mistakes won't stop you from keeping in touch with him. He's going to have a hard time letting go." The muscles in his tanned throat worked as he swallowed.

Everything in her softened as she allowed herself to feel the full force of love for him. This good man, so strong, so honorable, who wanted the best for his son and for her, was willing to put aside his own desires for their sakes. She reached over to lay a hand on his arm. "Actually, Nathan, I'm hoping he won't have to let go."

He frowned. "What do you mean?"

She took a breath. "I've been doing a lot of thinking since our talk in the barn. When Zach went missing, it brought everything into focus for me." She raised her eyes to meet his. "I realize now that it's impossible to lock all my emotions away and never allow myself to feel anything. That's not how God wants me to live."

Her knees trembled but she held herself firm. She needed him to know what was in her heart. "The truth is that I love you, Nathan. You *and* Zach. And I don't want to lose either one of you." Tears impeded her vision, making her unable to discern his reaction.

He covered her trembling hand with his. "You'll never lose our friendship, Paige. Are you saying you're ready for more than that?"

"Yes." It was the only word she could get out past the fear that rose up to choke her, but it was the only one she needed.

Nathan closed his eyes and said nothing. His lips moved silently, as if in prayer. When he opened his eyes again, a slow smile spread across his face. "Thank You, God."

He reached out to pull her into his arms and ever so slowly lowered his mouth to hers.

Joy filled her soul the moment his lips touched hers. This was where she belonged. In Nathan's arms, cherished and secure. Her heart fairly burst with all the love she'd repressed for so long.

When Nathan pulled back, he looked into her eyes. "I love you, too, Paige. So much it terrifies me at times. I thought I'd have to say goodbye to you tomorrow, and I didn't know how I was going to do that."

"You don't have to, not if you don't want to."

He stared. "What about your final year of school? You can't give that up now."

"No, but I can do most of the courses by correspondence." She smiled at him. "George has even offered me a deal on my room at the inn. Room and board in exchange for some clerical work and maybe some singing as part of the fall entertainment package."

Nathan's eyebrows rose. "You've already talked to George about this?"

She nodded. "This morning. I wanted to be prepared—just in case." She sobered. "I'm not presuming too much, am I? I know you and Zach are still grieving, and I don't want to overstep—"

He silenced her with a kiss that left her breathless. "When the time is right, I want nothing more than to make you my wife. Zach has already told me he wished you could be his mom."

She buried her face in his shoulder and inhaled the clean scent of his shirt. "I don't know how I deserved to find love a second time, but I do love you, Nathan. Very much."

"And I love you. Though I kept telling myself I had no business getting involved with anyone since I'd made such a mess of my life. Luckily, God had other plans for me."

She smiled, caressing his cheek. "For both of us."

Their lips met once more. Safe in the circle of his arms, the fear that had haunted her for years melted away, and she knew with absolute certainty that this was where she was meant to be. Paige raised a heartfelt prayer of thanks to God for helping her find her way at last.

Nathan pulled back, love shining in his eyes. "Wait till we tell Zach. This might be better news than a new puppy."

Paige laughed with him, a beautiful sound full of hope for the future. "Maybe so. If not, you might have to soften the deal with a pony!"

Epilogue

"Do I hafta go to school today?" Zach peered longingly out the window at the new fallen snow. "Maybe the school bus won't come and we'll have a snow day."

Paige laughed. "No such luck, pal. It's only a few inches. Now get your backpack. The bus will be here any minute."

With a begrudging sigh, Zach pulled his pack out of the closet and began to tug on his boots.

"Maybe we can make snow angels after school, provided your dad's home to look after your brother." In Paige's arms, the baby cooed as if he knew they were talking about him.

Zach wrinkled his nose. "When's Jake going to be old enough to make a snowman with me?" His biggest complaint about his brother was that Jake couldn't do anything yet.

"Oh, not for about another year or so. Until then, you're stuck with me and your dad."

"And Farley. He loves the snow."

She chuckled at the mental image of their black mutt romping through the white powder. "Yes, he does. Now scoot."

Paige kissed Zach goodbye and watched out the front door as he bounded through the fresh snow in the driveway to the waiting bus. She waved at Judy, the driver, before the noisy vehicle lumbered off.

"Well, Jakey. Looks like it's just the two of us."

In response, the baby rubbed a fist into blue eyes that matched his father's. Paige laughed and kissed the top of his silky head.

"Time for a nap, I think." Maybe she'd actually get to take a shower before noon today.

After putting Jake in his crib, she finished tidying the kitchen. She could hardly believe she and Nathan had been married for almost two years, and that Jake was already six months old. It amazed her how her life had fallen into place once she stopped fighting her feelings for Nathan.

They had married as soon as she graduated. Dan performed the ceremony with all her family and friends in attendance. It had been one of the happiest days of her life. The other was the day Jake was born.

Her career, or the lack of it, was the only snag in her otherwise perfect life. She'd managed to get some part-time work with a local psychiatrist, but it wasn't the calling she'd hoped for.

Then Jake had come along unexpectedly, changing all her priorities. She loved being a full-time mother to Zach and the baby, yet lately she found herself growing restless.

"Be patient," she'd told herself on more than one occasion. "I'm sure God has a plan."

After her shower, she did a load of laundry, fed Jake and was making herself a sandwich when she heard the front door open. She looked up in surprise when Nathan walked in.

"What are you doing home at this time of day?"

"Can't a man come home for lunch with his wife and son?" He smiled, bending to kiss her.

"Of course you can. We're happy to have your company." She laughed when he kissed Jake in his high chair and the baby smeared a grimy fist of applesauce across his nose. "Let me fix you a sandwich."

She turned back to the cutting board.

Nathan wiped his face, then took the knife from her hand. "That can wait a minute. I have some news first."

"What kind of news?" He was smiling, so she wasn't alarmed, only curious.

"Something that will please you, I hope."

She took the seat he pulled out for her, then waited while he sat beside her.

"Dan got a call this morning," he said. "We've finally been approved to start the youth center we've been talking about."

"That's great." She smiled at his enthusiasm, not really understanding why he had to come home to tell her this.

"Dan wants to expand the program. He's planning on hiring a youth counselor as a liaison between the church and the kids." He paused, grinning. "And he'd like that to be you."

Her eyes widened. "Me? A youth counselor?"

"It would only be a few hours a week—which would give you time for grief counseling, as well."

She frowned. "What grief counseling?" Her fondest wish, to help others suffering a loss, had yet to come true.

Nathan's grin widened. "That's the other good news. Dan finally managed to convince Mr. Dearling at the Pine Ridge Funeral Home that they need a grief-counseling program. Mr. Dearling has agreed, especially since Dan told him he has the perfect person in mind. He's even secured you a small office on-site."

As the idea began to sink in, a bubble of excitement rose in her chest. It was exactly the type of program she'd envisioned starting in New Jersey. "When would all this happen?"

"Whenever you feel ready to start working again. There's a lot of preliminary work to set up the youth program. But Mr. Dearling is prepared to have you start as soon as you're able."

Her mind reeling with a thousand jumbled thoughts, Paige pushed up from the table. "What about the kids? I'd have to find a sitter for Jake."

Nathan came up beside her and put his hands on her shoulders, calm and steadying. "All those details can be worked out as we go along."

Another thought struck her. "You wouldn't mind me going back to work? We agreed that I'd take a year off with the baby."

He took her face in his hands. "I know how important your career is to you, and I want you to be happy. Everything else will work itself out."

Sudden realization dawned at the look in his eye. "You put Dan up to this, didn't you?"

"I may have mentioned it a time or two." He dropped a light kiss on her lips.

Her heart swelled with love for this man who always had her happiness in mind. She wrapped her arms around him in a tight hug. "Thank you. You are amazing."

Once again, Paige marveled at how God answered her prayers once she let go and let Him take charge.

Jake whined to get out of his chair. She quickly unclipped the belt and lifted him out.

"Here, let me do the honors." Nathan reached for a washcloth.

Paige smiled at the tender way he cleaned his son's face and hands. "How did I ever get so lucky?" she whispered.

His gaze locked with hers, sending tingles along her spine. "Funny, I was thinking the exact same thing."

* * * * *

Dear Reader,

Inspiration for the setting of this story occurred while vacationing in the Muskoka region of Northern Ontario. My husband had rented us a rather "rustic" cottage, and in an effort to get away for an afternoon, we went on a drive and found a beautiful resort called Windermere House, which became the location for my story.

I already knew my heroine would be a grief counselor helping a young boy deal with the death of his mother. As most of you can likely attest, grief affects people in different ways. Some are swamped with guilt and anger, others retreat from life for fear of feeling such loss again. In my story, Paige turns to God for comfort and dedicates her life to easing the pain of others. Nathan, however, turns away from God, becoming paralyzed by misplaced guilt and anger.

I believe God brings people into our lives at the times we most need them: a friend, a coworker, a healthcare professional, a counselor. For Nathan and Zach Porter, that person was Paige McFarlane. By sharing God's unconditional love and forgiveness, Paige not only manages to heal her own grief, but finds the courage to risk falling in love again.

This story is very special to me, because in 2008, it became a finalist in the Golden Heart Contest®, giving me the first hint of success I'd experienced with my writing.

I love to hear from readers! You can reach me at sbmason@sympatico.ca, via my website www.susannemason.com or find me on Facebook.

Warmest regards & happy reading,
Susan

COMING NEXT MONTH FROM
Love Inspired®

Available February 17, 2015

A WIFE FOR JACOB
Lancaster County Weddings • by Rebecca Kertz
Jacob Lapp has loved Annie Zook since they were twelve years old.
Now that he's working at her father's blacksmith shop, will he finally get
the chance to forge their futures together?

THE COWBOY'S FOREVER FAMILY
Cowboy Country • by Deb Kastner
Rodeo rider Slade McKenna wants to protect his best friend's widow and
baby. As he helps the resilient single mom settle in on her ranch, he'll soon
get his own chance at family.

THE FOREST RANGER'S RESCUE
by Leigh Bale
Forest ranger Brent Knowles begins to fall for the teacher he's hired to
help his young daughter speak again. Can he reconcile his feelings when
his investigation into a forest theft threatens her family's livelihood?

FINDING HIS WAY HOME
Barrett's Mill • by Mia Ross
When prodigal son Scott Barrett returns home, he promises to stay out of
trouble. But soon he's in danger of losing his heart to the beautiful artist
he's helping restore the town's chapel.

ALASKAN HOMECOMING
by Teri Wilson
Returning home, ballerina Posy Sutton agrees to teach dance to the local
girls. When she discovers her boss is old sweetheart Liam Blake, can she
make room in her future for a love from her past?

ENGAGED TO THE SINGLE MOM
by Lee Tobin McClain
Pretending an engagement with ex-fiancé Troy Hinton to fulfill
her ill son's wishes for a daddy, single mom Angelica Camden finds
nothing but complications when she falls head over heels for the
handsome dog rescuer—again!
